JACKPOT

Everything That Glitters
Ain't Gold

TY A. PATTERSON

ISBN: 0998783102
ISBN 13: 9780998783109
Library of Congress Control Number: 2017903355
Ty A. Patterson, Jackson, MI

PREFACE

I WROTE THIS book because I had a revelation about how similar gambling was to relationships. The initial attraction is appearance. Some casinos are so immaculate that you almost can't wait to see the inside of them. Once you get in, the ambiance of a high-end casino gives you bright lights, music, shopping, great food and ringing machines. You immediately feel as if there is no other place you would rather be. When you stop looking and start to play a few slot machines, roll some dice or find some other interesting eye-catching game to try, reality sets in that nothing in the casino is free. *Not even the drinks.* You've got to pay to play and if you get caught up, not knowing when to cash out, you'll end up losing more money than you started with. I can't speak for both sides of the dating world but I'm sure women and men have experienced love at first sight. After you get past the nervous yet eager introductions you find yourself holding a conversation for hours with that special someone, and it seems like every word spoken is confirmation that it was meant to be. Somewhere in the relationship, you notice things that you don't particularly like, but you either ignore it or accept it. It may too-flirty behavior, a mean streak or just differences of opinions. When things spiral out of control, you find yourself talking and acting totally out of your character because you want to get things back to how they were; but you don't know how. Risks should end in lessons, not necessarily losses. So no matter if you're trying to win in life or in love, look beyond the surface. There may be rules, but it's not a game.

INTRODUCTION

A guy never knew how lucky he could be until he met Jasmine Jones. She was smart, beautiful, and ambitious, with a gorgeous petite frame, long and straight black hair, and brown eyes she often smiled with when people looked directly at her. For as long as she could remember she heard, *you sure are a pretty girl,* from her family, school teachers and people in passing. Jasmine wasn't heavy or thin, and she loved to wear embellished sandals on her size-six, pedicured feet. She rarely wore any jewelry, and guys often noticed her small, soft hands with nude polish and no rings. Her best quality always seemed to be a tie between her personality and her naturally alluring appearance. It was rare for her to be without male companionship. Guys were drawn to her. She had a very warm and sweet demeanor, and the dimple on the left side of her dollish face just added to her glow. Even though she acted modest on the outside, she was vain on the inside. She was kindhearted, but she was well aware that she was beautiful.

She knew how to present herself as the girl who could do no wrong, so there was an old-fashioned innocence about her that made guys want to make her smile. No gesture was too small for Jasmine, and she treated everything she was given like it was pure gold. Throughout her high school years, the gifts from guys got bigger, better, more sentimental, and more expensive. It was no surprise she was spoiled, and Valentine's Day became her favorite day of the year. Something about love, sweet cards, roses, and teddy bears never got old for her. Jewelry and money were always pleasant surprises as well but no matter how spoiled she was, Jasmine always believed it was the thought that counted. She smiled and laughed out loud at the love notes that jokingly stated, *I love you. Do you love me? Check yes or no.* Jasmine was very easygoing, and there wasn't too much she didn't enjoy during her free time with friends and family—gatherings at home, board games, cards, shopping trips, movie outings, slumber parties, and trips to any venue that had great music. But one thing she could not get into was gambling, which was why she didn't even like the arcade. Back in her teenage years, she didn't understand why her friends loved spending several dollars on arcade games and holding a million tickets only to win a key chain or maybe a cup. *Why not just go buy it from a store?*

Jasmine got older and still didn't like gambling, although she had always enjoyed the luxury of casinos. She thought they were absolutely dazzling. The fluorescent lighting, flamboyant colors, cascading water fountains, chandeliers, and unique designs always excited her. Everywhere she turned there seemed to be glitz and glamour as she marveled at the architecture and wondered how much it cost to build such a place. She wished she could one day have a house similar to what her eyes beheld—it seemed like paradise. She truly liked what she saw and how it made her feel. Everything was just beautiful and, in most cases, downright sexy. It made her want to dress up, look classy, and walk sassy because she was in the midst of money and excitement. The few times Jasmine played casino games, she never gambled more than twenty dollars because it was hard for her to quit after actually winning a few extra dollars. She knew just how addictive it could be. With every dollar, quarter, or nickel she dropped in, she usually won just enough to keep her sitting there but never hit it big. At the end of each visit, Jasmine always wished she had not wasted her money—money she worked hard for and could not get back. She figured she would have been fine enjoying the all-you-can-eat seafood buffet instead.

Her thoughts were always, *once I drop that money in the machine, it's gone. I might get it back, and I might not. At least with the buffet, the opportunities seem endless.*

When Jasmine was growing up, her mother always said, "Baby, it's better to have more than you need than to need more than you have." So having plenty was always the goal. Her mother explained, "Being pretty only goes so far. Take care of yourself so you ain't going around begging a man for nothing, or spending your money on him like a fool." Strangely her mother gambled in the casino all the time, not always winning. She dragged Jasmine along for the longest, most boring nights ever. She walked around the lobby for hours, even paging her mom over the intercom. As beautiful as those casinos were, she hated going at all if it meant staying too long. With every passing hour, everything about casinos that initially grabbed Jasmine's attention would all fade away by the end of the night. The lights suddenly were too flashy, the ringing noises got on her nerves, and the people she thought must have been rich—to sit and throw money away like that—all seemed to look like something was wrong with them. Her tired eyes went from person to person, finding ailments. *She's in a wheelchair. He has a mask on. That person over there is coughing up a lung. This person keeps scratching…*Jasmine just wanted to go home. It felt like visiting a hospital instead of a ritzy casino. However, she realized that just because those people were there for hours and hours, it didn't mean they were always successful. The ringing sounds made it hard to tell if people were really winning but it sure sounded promising. Jasmine was a bit confused about the experience and chose to simply enjoy the view as she pondered why people gambled at all. Maybe the busy atmosphere provided a distraction from what was really going on in their lives. People were putting all their cash and coins back into machines, spending their bill money, or losing their entire paychecks in hopes of a money miracle. Even after losing their money, real gamblers came right back with those same hopes. Jasmine thought those people were out of their minds, lazy, pitiful, out of touch with reality, and selfish. It still didn't make sense to Jasmine as to why people kept going back, not knowing if they would win or lose.

The only fond memory that stood out to her was meeting a cute light-skinned boy with green eyes who was wondering around the casino waiting on his dad. The boy noticed Jasmine, walked over to her, and gave her some of his quarters for the arcade. They discovered that they were both eleven years old and liked pizza, movies and swimming. He said his name was Will and wrote his phone number on the back of an empty gum wrapper that he had in his pocket. He was a slim boy with a corny sense of humor but very handsome. Luckily, Jasmine always kept a pen, a pack of gum, and lip gloss in her fanny pack that most people wore to casinos in the 90's. Hers was small with pink and purple sparkles, and she wore it around her waist and to the side. Will ended up moving several times and soon he and Jasmine lost touch. She missed running into him at the casino and she was stuck spending countless hours waiting on her mom to win or get sleepy so they could leave.

Years of this solidified why Jasmine Jones hating these casino trips—well, at least that's what she thought. She had no idea that, in many ways, she was just like the people she criticized while waiting for her mom. Jasmine was a sucker for sweet-talking, ambitious men with a chiseled body and a handsome face. She fell for it all so many times that her love life was like being on the Las Vegas strip. She spent years gambling and didn't even know it. Money wasn't on the table—it was her standards, integrity, trust, and ultimately her heart. The best thing Jasmine liked about dating, no surprise, was the variety of choices with every good-looking face, bright smile, and carefully shaped brown body she encountered. It was as if those bright colors, flashing lights, and bells of the casino were going off inside her head. Men, in her world, were like lottery tickets, slot machines, and gaming tables. Each was different yet equally fascinating, one more charming than the next, introducing the chance to win a soul mate. Images and sounds of promise drew her in, and enjoyment kept her there. She often thought of the casino lobbies with their smiling, friendly, lovely waitresses with exotic, appetizing foods and drinks.

What she didn't know was that, just like casinos, everything about dating had changed—the atmosphere, the players, and even the games. Nowadays money doesn't even drop from the slot machine anymore. You get a voucher showing what you won, while the machine makes a mechanical coin-dropping noise. To get your money, you must go stand in line and cash out your voucher. Most gamblers don't want to leave their locations, so they end up just spending their vouchers at the same machines. In essence they get lazy and fear losing their spot, even though they aren't winning. Jasmine would find out soon enough how this happens in relationships. With every twist and turn in the dating world, she still loved romance, and with Valentine's Day being her favorite holiday, the journey always seemed worth it. However, those journeys moved slower, were not as smooth, and didn't come as often. It didn't take long for her to realize that if she didn't stop what she was doing, she would lose her most valuable possession—Jasmine Jones.

Hitting the jackpot doesn't happen for everyone. But Jasmine learned it's achievable and very real unless one is afraid of taking chances, isn't willing to learn from his or her mistakes, or can't see past the surface of people. While it is true that some things aren't worth the risk, Jasmine had a lot to learn about true winning. Having a whole lot of nothing was the result of her penchant for quantity over quality in love.

JACKPOT

(A large prize that's offered for a specific outcome in a game)

I dedicate this to Victoria L. Jackson-Patterson.
Mom, I guess those days of being a bored little girl at Silverstar Casino in
Choctaw, Mississippi, finally paid off.

TABLE OF CONTENTS

CHAPTER 1

BEGINNER'S LUCK

(Unexpected success experienced by a person who is just starting a particular game)

So here I was—beautiful, young, intelligent…and living back at home with my parents in the rural country, one year left until obtaining my bachelor's degree.

But I had no choice. My parents had already warned me that after I graduated from college, I had to find a new address. I was almost twenty-one and my family's philosophy was "if you are old enough to vote and buy alcohol, then you are old enough to pay bills."

One day as I was sitting in my bedroom—yes, the one of my childhood—I heard my dad's monotone voice. "Jasmine, telephone."

I was so bored that summer I would have held a conversation with a bill collector—that is, if I had any bills.

"Hello?"

"Hi, how have you been? This is Will. Remember me?"

I only knew one Will in my entire life from the casino when we were little. He reminded me of the gum wrapper that he had written his name on. I had totally forgotten that I had three extra wallet-sized school pictures in my fanny pack that night and I have given him one. I was flattered but not shocked. I thought I was so gorgeous in those photos that I practically handed them out like business cards. I figured if I went on a school trip, I could leave some new cute guys with a souvenir-a picture of me. But a guy had to be super fine to get my phone number on the back. Will told me that he had been to college but he left to join the military. He was already a cutie from what I remember, and I could only imagine what the military had done to his physique.

"Of course I remember you," I said smiling. "What in the world made you think of me?"

"I never forgot you."

I was still the nice girl that he remembered when we were younger, but not as innocent. The conversations continued all summer, and I finally made a blind bet and agreed to meet up with him. We were eager to see each other, even though I was living in the country. If he could find my house in those outskirts, he would earn bonus points from me based on his survival skills alone. He found me, and his body was just as I had imagined—light, tight, and built just right. When we saw each other it was like those two kids from the casino arcade had reunited. There was so much to talk about with Will and it was a relief to know that he was still a polite young man, with that eccentric sense of humor, who happened to be single.

Soon it would be time for me to enroll in my last year of college and figure out what the heck to do with the rest of my life. Although Will was a pleasant surprise, he was stationed hundreds of miles away. Summer was over and I had to get back to reality. School, future goals, and economic hardship consumed me, while I was determined to party until after graduation whether Will was in the picture or not. *I didn't go after him, he came after me.* I had no idea that trying to have a long distance relationship in college would be such a recipe for disaster. I was single and super bored during the summer when Will called me, and by the time August came and I was back in school, it was like a movie director had appeared out of the backdrop of my life and yelled, "Action!"

I was living again—school, friends, parties—and this time I had Will as a boyfriend! It felt so good to turn down other male interests. The first two years of college without a boyfriend had some ups and downs. I mean, the guys came a dime a dozen, but the ones I wanted, I couldn't have. This wasn't high school. Everywhere in college were girls who seemed to have the choice guys on lock, and these girls were borderline crazy. I witnessed as girls paid for dates, let their boyfriends and cut-buddies drive their cars, and stayed in some crisis, fighting over these guys. Being a country girl living in a rural area, I wasn't used to any competition. I also wasn't used to these sorry college guys getting so much attention from the ladies. If they were "all that" why weren't these dudes in their apartments instead of a dorm room. Yet girls were chasing them down even after being cheated on, dissed in public, or even being beat up by their so called boyfriends. How was that even possible? Is this how the game goes in relationships? It was because the most popular guys were athletes, in fraternities, or were just fine as hell. They were popular and I admit, the companionship was fun at times, but it got old quickly. Thankfully I skipped out on the disarray, but seeing that role reversal made me sick. I decided a long time ago that I would rather be single than with a guy who came with headaches and heartaches. *So far, so good.*

I had a long-distance relationship with Will, but he refused to fade into the background just because he wasn't around physically. He pulled some strings with his contacts near me, and thanks to him, I landed a bank teller job that paid very well. I decided to use my school refund check to pay for the first months of my very first apartment, furniture, cell phone, and checking account. Receiving money from Will was the reason I even have needed a bank account. He sent me whatever I needed. Most of the time, he had to guess a dollar amount to send me because I hated asking for money. Truthfully I still don't. The "damsel in distress" type was never something I needed or wanted to portray. I could not stand the thought of pretending to be needy just to trick some unsuspecting guy into being drained and manipulated. Will supported me so much from a distance that, for the first time, I felt like an adult. I could not believe someone was willing to help me, without even seeing me or really knowing me for very long. For almost a year, I communicated with Will over the phone, and he was able to visit my new place once. At the time it was only fair that we become an "official" couple. He loved me, and he loved my dreams and aspirations. Most importantly, he was very family oriented and had a wonderful personality. It wasn't long before he completed his time with the military. We met each other's families and traveled together as the perfect couple. He even joined my church. Will never tried to move in with me because he was a true Southern gentleman. He picked me up for dates all the time, and yes, even though I had a place to myself, he respected that it was not his home. That did not stop him from coming to wash my clothes, help me cook, clean my dishes, and fix anything inside and outside my apartment. He even tried to wash my hair when I didn't feel like it. I don't think he really knew what he was doing, but it felt amazing and the simple fact that he tried was adorable. Will did it all. If I'd seen a T-shirt with *Lady Luck* across the front, I would have bought one in every color and worn them all the time to describe how things were going for me. From taking me to the best restaurants to buying me diamonds, Will made it happen by working nine-to-five at UPS just like I was taught a man should do. He had no kids, no drama and no debt, so his time was all about me. The problem was, I was also *all about me.*

Will had no problem lending me his car but my dad got me one so I could get used to making car payments. I was hardly ever home. Nearly every month I went on girls' trips or just partied every weekend. Will began to display signs of jealousy, although it was known in my social circle that I was not single but just hanging out. But as the saying goes, "When the cat is away, the mice will play." When I *was* home, I had no worries. Only I had a key to my car or to my apartment. "Having it all" became boring and stressful. I had to give my boyfriend a history lesson on every friend I had, especially male friends. When I joined my sorority he acted like I sold my soul to the devil and got a penis pass in return. As if it wasn't hard enough dealing with Will's remarks, his thoughts about guys in fraternities were kinda like the thoughts I used to have. I didn't want to admit that I understood why he was uneasy when I was around those guys. I just wanted him to trust me because I knew how to stop guys from going too far. The good thing was, I never had any problems in that area. However, it didn't help our relationship when the guys I thought I was done with were resurfacing left and right. Since my ex's were all so darn fine it was hard not to at least be friends with them again. *Hey, I didn't spend all those years at the casino without observing a few things, one of which was "Play to win".* There was no harm in a few friendships here and there as long as I made it clear that I was taken. I was not about to torture myself by cutting off communication with every guy I knew just to put Will at ease. If I so much as waved to a guy, the questions were coming.

"So just how many boyfriends have you had before me?"

"What? Boy, you so crazy."

"I'm just asking because you have a lot of male friends."

"Nah, I haven't had anything serious. These guys on campus are a trip."

"What about those frats guys that's always hugging you?"

"Oh! Those are just my brothers, babe. They don't look at me like that."

"You don't see *how* they look at you."

"Will, everybody knows I'm with you. I'm just waiting on *you* to know it."

Don't get me wrong—I loved being in a relationship and having Will all to myself, but as the years went on, I felt like I was put in a position I didn't ask for—the wife. It was ridiculous explaining the history of every single male I knew, and I just got tired of it. Pretty soon the exchange between Will and I went from thorough, to short, to "Don't even ask."

It felt like the more I lived life to the fullest in my relationship, the more Will tried to sabotage it so I could sit at home. It started with his suspicious attitude and soon his appearance started to go downhill. He stopped shaving, wearing cologne or getting hair-cuts, and if I mentioned anything about it, he assumed I was comparing him to my male friends or an ex. Instead of arguing, I'd just let it go. The fact of the matter is when Will dropped out of college he missed out on the things that I was so involved in. He wasn't just jealous of other guys, he was jealous of my entire college experience. Will and I continued to go on dates and to church, but I hated being seen with him because of how he carried himself. I figured it was some kind of test of my loyalty.

"Are you trying to embarrass me?" I frequently asked him at the beginning of any outing. He was dead wrong for trying to take me to fancy restaurants while looking like he was just some broken down negro I found on the street. On top of dealing with his untidy appearance, I had to look down or away every time a male passed by me to appease Will's insecurities and keep peace. I didn't want to talk to him about how I felt anymore because it was no use. I tried to end this jail sentence several times but I was too dependent on him. I always ended up needed him to fix something or pay for something else. On one hand he was a really sweet guy who probably didn't think I would be around as long as I had been. On the other hand, I wasn't as ready for a relationship as I had thought. Will looked for problems that initially weren't there, so I created reasons for him to doubt me. At the same time I kept calling on him because I was so used to him being there. He couldn't really prove that I was doing anything besides drifting away from him emotionally. I was guilty of playing games. I was thinking, *OK, you want me to be imperfect—so be it!*

I was tired of being sheltered for no reason. I just wanted a boyfriend, not a husband—and certainly not a jealous one who didn't keep himself up. I realized the flowers he used to send me "just because" now came to apologize for his behavior.

Thinking back, I never really got to know him. He had come into my life when I was about to leave the nest of my parents' house, and because I felt like he saved me, the least I could do was make him "the one." I realized that just to keep him close, I had become the very same stereotype that I hated-the "damsel in distress". *Damn.*

In the beginning Will and I got along great, and I never felt threatened. I felt secure, like having just-in-case money for emergencies. There is nothing that he would not do for me. I knew I was treasured, but I wasn't in love. I wasn't even in lust. I was in a lie. I used his monetary support as an excuse to stay in a relationship. Nothing about him made me smile anymore. Over time all the small things about him I didn't necessarily like became utterly repulsive. Every time he lit a cigarette, I dreaded the sour smoked-out kisses I had to endure, and I immediately became disgusted. His clothes never fit right, and the colors were always some depressing shade of military brown or green. I don't even know what kind of shoes he was wearing all the time. I would look down at his feet and shake my head thinking, *what are those?* I could not force myself to laugh at another of his lame jokes, and for goodness' sake, when was he going to get a haircut? We still tried to make it work, because he was taking care of me. One time I told him I couldn't skate, and he took me on a date to an ice rink. I thought it would be romantic, but instead he got frustrated because I didn't glide around like an Olympic gold medalist. I couldn't believe Will had the nerve to scream at me like he was having a basic training flashback.

I finally blurted out, "Oh, hell no! Take me home! You really know how to take the fun out of anything!" I wasn't happy about it at all, and his apologetic gestures became even more annoying as I reached a boiling point of pure repulsion. I never took into consideration that after years of military life dealing with demands, repetition, training, discipline, restraint, and even losing people close to him, some of his habits were hard to break. When I think back to that terrible skating date, I believe he was mad because I wouldn't fall. I was trying to be cute, and I was not about to be embarrassed. This relationship had turned into a misfortune. Because Will came along during a new turning point in my life as the answer to all my problems, I assumed that over time I would see him as the perfect match for me—my jackpot. I thought, *if he's "the one," I'll never even wonder about another guy.* The idea of security was all that could come from this situation. I wanted it to work, but I wanted so many things about him to change. When that didn't happen, I stopped caring about how I made him feel. Since my attempts to move on were not effective, I wanted him to dump me. I was not at all ready for how the chips were about to fall. I did a lot of road running with my friends, and I encouraged him to do the same. He was around too much, and it seemed he didn't really have a life of his own. After all the little vacations I had gone on with or without him, he finally decided to go visit an army buddy. I hoped his hanging out with friends might put some spark back into his personality, so of course I was happy to see him go out and have fun. I had seen all his army pictures, and I appreciated that he shared those memories with me, but a large part of me still wanted him out of my life.

"Make sure you have fun, and take pictures," I told him while he was in the airport.

"I'll try. I love you, Jasmine," he said before hanging up his cell phone.

I don't recall everything I did while he was away, but I am sure it involved my friends, alcohol, monopoly, a card game, and probably a dude here and there. This was the first time in a couple of years that Will was away from me, but we talked on the phone frequently the entire time he was gone. However, his calls were abnormally short—a few minutes at a time. Even though I missed him a little, it wasn't enough to care. It didn't hit me until later that his calls were almost like "hi" and "bye" in the same sentence.

A few days after he returned, he came to my apartment, and his whole demeanor was very gloomy. He tried to act like his normal quirky self, but something wasn't right. Something had happened while he was gone, but I didn't know what. So what did I do? If you are assuming I asked a bunch of questions or even searched his phone, you are absolutely wrong. Instead I was extremely nice and overly sensual, and I wore clothes that made his mouth water and head spin. I did all the things I knew how to do before we met, like cooking and cleaning, and I catered to his every wish. He showed me a few pictures from the trip, but I knew there should have been more. Whatever happened on his trip ate away at his conscience like a piranha, until he ended up in tears and finally spoke up.

"Jay, I have something to tell you."

"Sure, what is it, babe? I was about to ask if you lost a bet or something. How are your old army buddies doing?"

His words rushed toward me like a mob of gangsters, and the showdown began. "I didn't go see an army buddy. An ex-girlfriend from the military paid for that flight so I could see her. We were engaged at one time, but she was stationed out of the country. We never officially broke up. It just ended."

Wait...what? I knew it. As much as I wanted those words to go back into his funky nicotine contaminated mouth, where they had come from, I had to ask the next question.

"Are you referring to that ugly, bony, black-ass bitch who was sitting on your lap in the photos you forgot to hide?" I asked with a nice-but-nasty smile.

"Yes," he said, his head down.

Will didn't know that the day he returned from that trip, I went to his house to see him. I was in the middle of washing and folding his clothes but when I cleaned off the coffee table there were pictures hidden under some books. I never said a word, even though he was in the next room.

So, I waited for him to defend her in some way or at least express some emotion for her, but he never did. I had to act angrier than I was, because the truth was that I totally understood why it had happened-he had needed closure with his ex-fiancé. But being understanding wasn't my job. My job was to be mad as hell and act a damn fool.

"Then we agree that she is black, bony, and ugly, so what did you do? And by the way, she is a ratchet slut too because she knows you are in a relationship. Did you two whores rekindle the flame?"

"No. I know I shouldn't have gone. I'm sorry!"

"This is why you are so suspicious of me. *You're* the one being sneaky. Get the hell out!"

By then I was making myself yell. He stood up to leave so I stood up. I followed him to the door screaming louder and louder until he had gotten right outside of my door. When he turned around for the last time, I slapped him and slammed the door in his face. I ran into my room rambling and throwing things. As he went to his car, he looked up at my window only to see any and everything of his being thrown out onto the stairs and into the parking lot. I wasn't even that mad but I kinda enjoyed that episode. I had been trying to get out of the relationship anyway, and I needed a reason. I admit it did sting that he cheated on me, but his screw up was my way out. After that moment with Will, I believed that no matter what a guy showed you, he was never strong enough or loyal enough to be faithful. The bad part was that I didn't want to go straight back to being single, because I didn't have any definite options. So I kept pretending to be furious for a long time, and this, of course, gave me time to date anyone and everybody. Then when I got ready, I acted as if I was over what Will did, and I started answering his phone calls. After much begging and more money being spent on me we got back together but he didn't know he was one of many. Will assumed that if I took him back, it must be a sign we were meant to be.

I didn't give him a tangible reason not to trust me. He saw the sweet side of me and the past situation was never brought up again. I think he broke a record with the number of dates we had, flowers he sent, and gifts he'd given me on holidays and special occasions, but I knew I didn't want to stay with him.

The only reason our relationship seemed to be mending was because I quickly labeled him as a cheater and continued doing what I wanted with no remorse. This was all the ammunition I needed to date other guys that I had put on hold when I was off the market in college. One particular year as Christmas approached, I knew I would get extravagant gifts from Will, and I wasn't even excited. I was used to receiving material things from him, and it all meant nothing to me. It felt like he was literally paying for his mistake with the money he spent on me. The holidays came, and we were on one of our many top-notch dinner dates, and on the way home, it happened. He actually asked me to marry him. The ring was beautiful and precisely what I would have wanted. It had rows and rows of diamonds, but I didn't want this from *him*. From day one he cared more about me than I cared about him. It could have worked out, but I didn't want it to. So that same night, I left him and the ring. The four-year relationship was over, and I finally said goodbye to the Will, the UPS man. On the outside I felt like I had broken even, but actually, in the midst of my selfishness, I lost my trust and my confidence.

CHAPTER 2

WILD CARD

*(A playing card that can have any value, suit, color, or
other property in a game at the discretion of the player
holding it)*

I knew it wouldn't be hard to find love again, because I was still
dating. But Will had set the bar rather high as far as what I
knew I could have in a guy. He had to be handsome, physically
fit, and financially helpful, and he had to be a churchgoing man
who thought the world revolved around me. Guys often came
after me, and that was how it was supposed to go. *Girls don't chase
guys; guys go after the girls—end of story.* Besides, I really needed to
take a break. I was enjoying life and the friendships that had de-
veloped in college, one in particular. After I received my special-
ist degree in marketing, I was promoted to branch manager at
the bank and had to attend a training session in Nevada. My coworkers and I stayed at Harrah's Lake Tahoe hotel and casino. I

packed my bags and called my friend to let him know I would be in his area. Well, Trey wasn't just a friend, but I still don't quite know what to call him. At times he seemed like a best friend, but I didn't see him often enough for that. It wasn't technically a romantic relationship, but it was mighty close. I knew him before I started dating Will, and it became the perfect time to reach back and pick up where I left off with Trey. I was so content being with him and there was nothing we couldn't talk and laugh about. Likewise, there was nothing we couldn't do together and still remain tight like skinny jeans on a hippo. We never had one disagreement. We had only laughs and conversations, which turned into date nights, which turned into breakfast. So you get the picture. With Trey, it wasn't about any gifts, Prince Charming antics, or sappy heart-melting moments. This dude was extremely spontaneous, not to mention straight up hilarious. Just because he was a homey/lover/friend didn't mean my demeanor changed to match his. As close as we were, I was not about to be around him in a T-shirt and sneakers. Seeing him, meant a trip to the salon, the nail shop, Victoria's Secret, and a new purchase of stilettos. Trey didn't ask for all that, but I gave it to him. He came to visit me at Harrah's and he let me know that he was still single. He lived a little farther than I would have liked but I wasn't trying to be a homey this time. I was ready see where we could take our friendship now that I was single. Hell, he was always single. After we met at Harrah's the visits continued. He was always at my apartment and I was at his. Each trip we took to see each other brought us closer. I started to get attached and paid extra attention to every detail about myself, because when I saw Trey, he was always so neat in a laidback kind of way. He was not suit-and-tie clean but ready-for-any-event-or-activity clean. He was just always ready. True enough, there wasn't a side of me he hadn't seen, but I didn't want get too comfortable in my appearance just because we were friends. I often wondered why we were never in a more serious relationship. I met him during our college days of partying and having fun. But the more time I spent with Trey, I saw what I wanted to see even though I wasn't always showing what I needed to show. I found myself wanting to be his girl but I didn't show him girlfriend potential. I showed up as a friend with benefits, and just like an even money bet, I got what I wagered for—friendship. He didn't even appeal to me when I first saw him years ago, because he just wasn't my type. I guess I was hooked on his personality. Just like how Steve Urkel of TV's *Family Matters* went into that transformation chamber and came out as Stephan Urkel, Trey went from kinda cute… to handsome…*that muthafucka is fine.* He was a lot taller than me, built like a basketball player, and had a nice milk chocolate color. He always wore hats that almost covered his glasses and flirty-brown eyes. As silly as he was, he never smiled really big. He just had a sexy grin and a baritone voice that gave me chills. Trey was my wild card. He could flip and become whatever I wanted, from a joker to a king. When we indulged in a night of jazz, wine, and poetry, he felt like a confidant. When we crossed paths at a party, bumped and grinded on the dance floor, talked noise all night, and then went our separate ways, he was my boy toy. If I wanted movies, snacks, and laughter, he was a sweet date. If all I wanted to do was vent about life and think back on old times, he was a buddy who didn't mind strolling with me down memory lane. If I wanted a midnight creep, he was

Dr. Feel Good. My mind and heart turned him into Mr. Right. Sadly, just because I would spent time with him like this for several years, it didn't mean he looked at me as more than a friend. I was so caught up in these back-and-forth weekend flings that I didn't want to mention getting serious to him. And when I did, I wasn't ready for the truth.

"Wow," he said. "I didn't know you saw me like that. I'm flattered, but I hate the long-distance thing. I tried it once, and it was horrible. I don't even think I'm ready to be in a relationship, but I'm glad you told me how you feel. If only you lived closer."

I could have gotten mad and reacted terribly to what he told me, but I didn't. It was the truth. I told myself my options were to continue seeing him as a "friend with benefits" and have a great time knowing a relationship was not in the forecast *or* be angry at his honesty and cut him off.

I had absolutely nothing else going on other than working at that bank, and this guy did nothing wrong but tell me how he felt. Did he care about me? Yes. Was he in love with me? No. Did he want to continue seeing me? Hell yes. I knew if we parted ways, his life would still go on, so my decision was to keep the dice rolling. I changed how I looked at him and my thoughts went back to the friendship zone. From then on he was back to being my ace, my homey, and my brother. There were no hurt or awkward feelings. If anything, we seemed to get closer because I handled the truth without thinking he was a bad guy for not wanting a committed relationship. He was everything Will was not. Trey had confidence and modesty like I'd never seen, and he had superb taste in everything. He was polite, always considerate, and very social. He stayed on the go because he loved to travel and carried himself very well. He could hold a conversation with anyone about anything and was not jealous. He often had the spotlight but didn't ask for it. He was open-minded about trying new things and going to new places, and he had patience. His calmness drove me crazy in a delightful way, and I was always excited to be around him even if we did nothing but lay in each other's arms and listen to neo-soul music. Everything he wore, drove, said, or did was perfect. The way I felt about him was so strong that if he coughed or sneezed, I was saying "Bless you" and thinking *"Aww, how cute."* His kisses could put Cupid's little ass right out of business. Even as friends, when we were near each other, there was an undeniable magnetic pull. He was single, and so was I. I didn't *really* want him to ever get that sister-brother vibe with me. We were the type of friends that could be mistaken for a couple. But others' assumptions, especially from my friend Ashley, made me revisit the thought of love quite often. Ashley's frequent phrase *ya'll look cute together,* was keeping my feelings and me in the game. I pretended to have let those strong feelings go. I was in love with this guy, but I would rather have him as a friend than nothing at all. Time went by, and I was with him at least every other weekend. We burned up some miles going back and forth, but it was worth every minute. We went to the movies, parties, casinos, restaurants, and the circus. I remember one weekend, going to the fair and watching him play basketball just to win me something. He finally won a stuffed animal for me. It was a big cute turtle that we decided to name June Bug. To Trey these were probably just silly times and fun outings, but I had never been in such a thrilling situation before so it was a whole new experience for me. I don't recall having as much fun with Will, much less having him win me a stuffed animal at a fair. The typical fun dates I had never experienced before with Will came easily with Trey. It wasn't that he was like a big kid, but he just lived life with a smile. He never let anything bother him or get him upset. Trey was easygoing, and I was captivated.

"What you got up for the weekend?" he frequently asked.

"You tell me," I'd say with a smile.

"It's so much going on here, you should come if you can. I can go ahead and check out what's happening, plan some things, and e-mail you the events."

"Never a dull moment with you, huh? That's what's up."

"You know me, Jasmine. Plus the weekend ain't long enough. Gotta plan."

"Ha-ha…I know. All I gotta do is show up and show out, huh."

"Fa-sho."

My visits to see him turned it into road trips with my friends. It was nothing for all of us girls to catch a flight especially since one of our mutual friends worked at the airport. When my girls and I reached our destination, I went my way with Trey and they went theirs. On the way home, my friends and I always met back up, blushing with all kinds of hot steamy rundowns of how our escapades went.

"So what did you do?" we'd ask each other.

"You don't wanna know," I'd replied.

"Jasmine, you mean we *already* know about you," someone would say.

"Yeah, yeah…but tell us anyway, Jay!" Ashley would say.

"Nah, somebody else can go first," I insisted.

"Well, I'm going last. I don't wanna put ya'll heffas to shame," said another.

That's pretty much how it went. We all had something to say, just being girls, being happy and all playing games. Not one time was I ever ready to leave Trey, because time flew by when we were together. His goodbye hugs were so warm and long that I almost cried on many occasions. I couldn't think of a bad moment with him. I had the best of both worlds. He was a friend with a listening ear, as well as a guy who was interested in me and wanted to make every moment better than the one before. Anybody who knew him knew that he was the life of the party. He was definitely an entertainer, but when it came to me, the curtains closed and it was just the two of us—no mess, no lies, and no worries. We had been friends for so long that I could have spotted him in a million-man march. College homecoming was always something I looked forward to. We didn't plan to see each other outside of the homecoming festivities because had so many other people to reunite with, but Trey always ended up with me before the weekend was over. During that time, even if we ended up at the same party or event, I never initiated conversation, even if I saw him first. I was still playing games. I wanted him to approach me with his silly over-the-top hugs and gestures. Without fail, he always did. Any stranger would have thought we were the perfect pair of hearts. He would go back to his friends across the room, and I would go back to my friends only to hear the same thing. I knew the question was coming.

"Why don't ya'll just hook up?" a mutual friend asked. "You do everything else couples do."

I smiled and laughed, *I knew it.* "No, we don't need to hook up. We're just friends, and I'm fine with that. He's single, I'm single, and we have no problems," I explained.

"Ain't too much more *hooking* ya'll can do. Both of ya'll are playing games." said Ashley.

"Exactly, no problems! What's stopping you two, Jasmine?" asked another.

"If it's distance, Jay, you better pack your bags and move!" said Ashley.

I assumed if outside people thought this, surely by now he did too. The only thing we didn't do together was attend church. On Sundays one of us was usually heading back home, so there wasn't much time for that. It was as if I couldn't picture being with anyone else. At one point I pictured myself with him forever. *Yes, I would hit up one of those Vegas chapels and get hitched.* Being with him was indeed addictive. I could be at home, think of him, and smell his cologne out of nowhere. My mind was that wrapped up. Do people still say "sprung"? That's what I was. My thoughts were always, *what in the world could be keeping this man from being mine? Doesn't he know he struck gold with me? I don't make him plan these dates and trips. He does it because he wants to. He enjoys being with me just as much as I enjoy being with him.* That last part he told me, and he never lied to me, so I still thought, *we see each other so much. Being a couple was almost a given.* I wanted to wait until he suggested a relationship. Until then, I continued like things were perfect between with Trey. I never stopped to see the time I was wasting or how available I had made myself.

One day, slowly looking around my apartment, I realized I didn't have one gift from him—no bear, flowers, jewelry, or anything to show for the entire friendship. I had no money in my hands from him, not one card, and not even a freakin' T-shirt! *Aw hell, what am I doing?* I thought I was winning but I didn't figure in this negative expectation when I was playing the rush. I knew Trey wasn't really romantic—just amazingly adventurous, courteous, and very respectful. It became obvious he still wasn't in love with me. As busy as his real life was, he was still available for me, like, all the time. Or was I the one available? Trey didn't have just one job. He just did whatever he wanted to until his time ran out. He worked many temporary and seasonal jobs because he liked his freedom and he got bored easily. I had no issue with that because I reaped the benefits of his impulsive adventures. He had a knack for making me feel special, in a way nobody else did. But I realized that just because we saw each other more and more, it didn't mean his feelings had changed. He was enjoying the moments, without consideration for a future—well, at least not with me. I had led him to believe I was happy with how things were, and in fact I was miserable. I hated the drive back from visiting him, and I hated when he had to leave me and return home.

He always reminded me, "Man I wish you could stay longer. There's a lot to do here."

I laughed. "Oh, really now? I know but it's not like you won't be visiting me soon. Besides, you will find *a lot to do* regardless when I am around. "

"Fa sho. Girl, you just got some good….uhh cookies."

"Whatever, Trey. Just give me a call later and we'll pick up where we left off."

"Already."

"See ya soon, Cookie Monster."

I'd wanted Trey to replace Will. That would have been so perfect. Because I was not Trey's girlfriend, He spent money on me but he wasn't getting me any material things but maybe he assumed buying me gifts would give me the wrong impression. He gave me experiences and memories instead. I battled inside my head, trying to define and dissect what Trey was doing. But it really wasn't hard to explain. He was single. We were friends with benefits, no strings attached. I knew that if I chose to throw in the cards and end this game, he would not argue with me about it because he wasn't confrontational. Whatever I wanted to do was always fine with him. This also meant he wouldn't fight to keep me around. The confusing thing was that whenever other guys expressed interest in me, he gave them the "don't even try it" speech. He didn't want me, but nobody else could have me either. That was some sneaky double-standard foolishness. First of all, I made my own decisions about whom I did and didn't date. Second, I would have never dated any friends of his anyway-well, not on purpose. He should have known that. I had to leave Trey alone or otherwise keep gambling with my time. The decision wasn't a tough one since there was no progression in the relationship. I got a fixed amount of affection from him, no matter how close we seemed to get. And just like with Will, Trey became less and less appealing to me. Nothing he said was funny anymore. Nothing he did impressed me. We called it quits and went our separate ways.

I won't lie—it hurt worse than breaking my engagement with Will. I thought that if I didn't nag Trey about a deeper relationship, I would get one. However, he was already getting everything from me, so why would he bother? He had a royal flush. Many times I wonder, with all that travel, if he ever filled up my gas tank. Was I was too high on him to notice? Then again, he probably did, and I am just being petty. When I think back on the time wasted, I always pinpoint the things he didn't do. But it was no use, because the good outweighed the bad in my mind. Trey made me feel great in so many ways. Yes, I had the time of my life with him. But if I didn't get so much as a birthday card from him, how the heck was I supposed to get a commitment? *Crap. I should have just stayed with Will and stocked up on breath mints. I could be planning a wedding by now, and I know it would be extravagant.* Will was in love with me. Why didn't Trey see the same beautiful, special, rare, wife-to-be Will saw? Trey was trippin'. He must not have known I was almost married and that a line of guys was waiting for me to give them a shot, including his so-called friends. I knew Will was still waiting for me to change my mind. I figured Trey must have had some skeletons, bad habits, and a few loose screws he didn't want to admit to, and maybe a platonic friendship was his escape from how messed up he must have been. Whatever his problem was, it wasn't me. There was no way he would ever find another girl like me. I could get another guy like him in a heartbeat. It was his loss, and I made myself almost hate him for telling me the truth.

I stopped speaking to him for a long time, but I missed him. New friends and experiences came along, and pretty soon I was back to my old habits and wasting time with guys from my past. But all it took was for me to cross paths with Trey again, and I was right back at that slot machine. He wasn't mad at me and never questioned why I had let it all go before. He was simply there when I decided he meant more to me than I had wanted to acknowledge. Even though we had separations and times when we fell back into each other's arms, his mind was made up. I was going back to him like an obsession. I had such a great time with him, and my friends had grown in love with the idea of us as a couple. I did everything I could to change his mind, but we ran our course and I could tell that he had met someone else-I could feel it. Trey and I had been friends for seven years, but there was nothing lucky about that number. He still called to check on me, and he never went without telling me Happy Birthday, but when I called or texted back, he didn't respond. After I settled on just being his friend forever, this time Trey pulled the plug. I knew that was the end. There was no argument, no friction, no goodbyes… and no friendship. When he decided to stop, he stopped—just like that. I couldn't stand him for the way he left, but I was surely going to miss him.

I felt like he had robbed me. But whatever I felt like he took, I gave it away freely. I went from being hurt to angry all over again. *Surely this negro is going to end up single for the rest of his life, not to mention miss the heck outta all this. Cookies or no cookies, I was the perfect match for him, and he knew it. Screw him!* I hoped the next chick he got with would be hell on wheels. This one set me back pretty badly since I should have ended the chase when I had the chance. I wanted to get back what I had given to him all along—my time and my heart.

CHAPTER 3

PLAYING PAIRS

(Playing two cards of the same denomination)

I was enjoying my job as branch manager and I was doing very well for myself. The next thing on my agenda was to be a financial advisor. Of course I kept a poster on my wall that stated, "It is better to have more than what you need, than to need more than what you have." *Thanks momma.* That was my personal slogan that I used as a signature on emails and my business cards at my desk. The job was pleasant but I never really socialized at work, unless someone stopped by or when we had team meetings and office parties. Just because I wasn't talking didn't mean I wasn't looking. Quite a few times, a specific person returned my glances each time he came to our branch office. Clearly he was in a higher position than I was, because he never seemed to be doing any work. He just walked around, wearing a suit. He was not my type at all, but he carried himself in a particular way that demanded attention, and he certainly got it. I shouldn't have even had a type being that I was still single. Will and Trey looked nothing alike, but at least they were taller than I was. This guy was kinda short, but he had ace of spades, midnight-black skin that looked like he came straight off a Jamaican beach. If I had never heard him speak, I would have guessed he had an accent. *And braids?* I hated braids, no matter who wore them. If a guy didn't keep a fresh haircut, I figured he was lazy, broke, or maybe he was just from another country. Not many guys worked in my office, so I looked forward to seeing him walk by my door…perhaps on purpose. I had to figure out who he was; his title; and, of course, where his desk was so I could eventually return the favor of simply walking by. I don't know why I never noticed him before, but this deep dark piece of chocolate could dress his tail off. *A businessman!* I doubted he owned a T-shirt or gym shoes. *Wait a minute—is he a pretty boy who thinks every female in the building is watching him? I hope not.* Betting limits were already coming into my head, but I came to my senses and snapped out of it. I was at work to work—nothing more, nothing less. I didn't have time for some shiny, shea-butter-smelling, arrogant, wanna-be-seen guy who thought I was going to be one of his cubicle groupies. *I don't know him, but to hell with him—yes, already.* I had gotten an attitude just that quick for no reason. I had a full argument in my head, with myself, about a complete stranger. That stranger walked past my office, wearing a hint of cologne intense enough to have me roll my chair away from my desk to follow it. It was like I had spotted a new sparkling slot machine and was ready to play again. He turned around.

"You need something?"

"Oh no, I'm fine, Mr...."

"Carter. That's my first name."

He gave me a look as if to say, *Yes, I can see you are very fine*, but I was embarrassed that he had caught me looking.

"Mr. Carter I have been seeing a lot of you lately. Do you work in this building?"

"I actually do. I am a new loan officer here. Normally I just use the back door by the parking lot."

"Oh ok. Well, as you can see, I am right in the front. Couldn't hide if I wanted to.

The next thing I knew, passing by evolved into exchanging e-mails and eventually phone numbers. This guy was nothing like I had thought he would be. I had known him only in the work environment, but his demeanor was very subtle, intimidating, and mysterious. Actually I felt nervous around him, and that made me even more curious. It seemed he had unreachable high standards, but that didn't stop me from playing along. I usually dressed cute but casual for work because I was always on the phones, but I changed my wardrobe to catch his eye. I tried my best not to wear the same thing twice when I thought I would see him. That took some strategy, since I was living paycheck to paycheck. Without Will to help me around the house, I really didn't have money to play with. But this guy's appearance certainly influenced me to pay more attention to my mine. I typically looked decent, but for some reason I now wanted to look nearly perfect even on my worst day. He definitely noticed. Carter never once said anything less than flattering to me, and I wanted to keep those compliments coming by any means necessary. It was hard work, but it paid off. For a while our talks stayed on the professional side. We spoke about work and had a few laughs, but too many people were in my building, and I didn't want to deal with whispers or funny looks. I tried to keep my distance but he made that very difficult.

"May I sit with you?" he asked from behind me.

"Yes, you may."

I was in a rush, eating by myself, as usual, in the employee break room. I took half-hour lunches just so I could clock out thirty minutes early.

But I went back to hour lunches because I loved sharing Carter's company. We weren't making googly eyes at each other, and no flirting or provocative words were exchanged but even an hour wasn't long enough when we had lunch together. I looked forward to his spiritual references and Bible scriptures. He often told me about the church services and Bible studies that he attended and I learned that he was a youth pastor. I was very impressed and I gladly accepted his invitation to church. When Monday came I was always uplifted at work instead of sluggish. Carter is the reason I stopped drinking coffee. He *was* my coffee. Even with all the good things about him, I still had my doubts. I never saw him talking too long with many females at work, and that made me wonder if he was interested in men. Nothing was wrong with him. Carter just believed in making time for the woman he wanted—not necessarily the women who wanted him. We had awesome conversations each time the opportunity came, so I became even more interested in him. I felt like he was choosing me. He was so professional and obviously had a lot of self-control, but we were purposely in each other's presence daily. I was tired of acting like I didn't want to know him outside of work, but I wasn't about to make the first move. I started to receive little post it notes under my keyboard from him. That was the cutest thing to me—those notes. His demeanor was inno-cent...yet very direct. His notes were always full of compliments about me—from my hair to my shoes. But I wondered if he cared only about my looks. Then I got another note from him that read, *'I hope this note makes you smile the way I do when I think of you. There is something about you that intrigues me and I have to move on my feelings. You just do something to me. I am not seeing anyone and if you are single I would love to get to know you exclusively. You look gorgeous today and every day. Jasmine, I want you.'* So the dating began, and I felt like a high roller again. I always thought I could avoid workplace romances, but I had never met a guy quite like this. Carter was more than I expected. I had no idea how much fun an intelligent businessman could be. Day by day he was a walking mural of blazers, suits, ties, tailored slacks, designer shoes, briefcases, sensual cologne, and a hint of cocoa butter—I knew cocoa butter when I smelled it. But this same guy was also funny and fun to be around, and he was incredibly sweet and attentive. What won me over was that he was very active in the church. He had me beat on that. *Could it be I have met a combination of Will and Trey? I've doubled up on my luck, for real!* Carter's voice was so suave that when he spoke, I swore I saw the sunset, ocean water, and flowers that blew in the wind. Yes, his voice sounded that good—even deeper than Trey's. I listened to him speak to irate people at work, and it was like he could calm a raging sea with his words. His smooth dark skin reminded me of bittersweet chocolate. Yes, he was very debonair on the outside but a down-to-earth country guy who didn't mind work. When he visited me, he always asked what I needed done. He put those long locks of his in a ponytail, threw on a white T-shirt and jeans, and found odd jobs to do at my home or to my car. Once again a man was taking care of me—mopping, washing clothes and bringing me groceries. I thanked Jesus out loud when I saw him working underneath my car to fix it. I practically caught the Holy Ghost when Carter was doing my dishes. *I hated doing dishes.* I hadn't been treated like this in years. In the beginning I was sure I had him figured out. I thought he was stuck-up, self-centered, and didn't even like women. I was so wrong. He was just a regular man, who often got his hands dirty. And he happened to be perfectly groomed, charming, and fine when he wasn't getting grease under his nails. He knew how to handle himself, and he put thought into everything he did or said before making any sudden moves. Carter was ambitious and often asked me about my short- and long-term goals, because he had several. I can honestly say that was a first. Guys who came into my life knew I was talented and creative, but they never focused on it or pushed me to fulfill my dreams. Our talks about future business plans, money making ventures and life goals seemed to arouse him. A blend of beauty and brains was a major turn-on to him. I had thought he was attracted only to beauty, but again I was wrong. This man was about being in the moment, but he also had a healthy outlook about the future. He was fearless when it came to the pursuit of success in finances, spiritual well-being and happiness.

He was handsome, funny, thoughtful, handy, intelligent, and sweet. He was also very generous. I called on him many times to help me out of bad situations. My car kept breaking down, my finances weren't right, and sometimes I just needed food and a foot rub. This was no difficult task for him. He confessed to a foot fetish and described my feet as "a perfect shade—not too light, not too dark, no marks, and pretty toes."

This perfect gentleman never once tried to push up on me the wrong way. I wondered if he had a girl on the side, but we had gotten so close that I knew better. We were still just friends, but he was making great deposits with his constant notes, compliments, and conversation. One autumn evening after work, I clocked out and was headed to my car when he came after me in the parking lot to verbally express how he felt about me. He confirmed that he was single and having serious feelings for me. He wanted to be sure I was single and that the feeling was mutual before getting too attached. I breathed a sigh of relief. I smiled and welcomed his heart, and he hugged me. I reached up and touched his braids, which were bundled into that beautiful ponytail. In his embrace I knew more was coming because he wouldn't let go. I smelled that sweet hint cocoa butter. It was sweet, and he was warm. He looked at me and kissed my forehead. Then he leaned his head to one side and kissed my cheek. He flashed the prettiest white smile ever and kissed me in a way that made time stand still. At that moment I was all in. I had pushed all my chips to the table, and I was ready to win. Part of me hadn't thought of him in a physical sense, because he wasn't a big tall guy. I kinda didn't expect much from him physically. *What could his lil' self possibly do with me?* That one kiss felt like sex. *Hmm… assumptions will make a fool out of you if you let 'em.* Nothing could have prepared me for how he finally unleashed his romantic attraction. I will say he made all my lights, bells, whistles, and flashes ring out. He took me to Treasure Island and Pleasure Island, all at the same time. What a payout! He often ran his braided hair along every part of me, and it smelled so good and felt breathtaking. If the females at work knew the new scent in his hair came from my body, they would have stopped asking to touch it. It didn't make me jealous, but it made me laugh. *Silly broads.*

It was a mutual decision not to make an announcement about us at work, because "what happens in Vegas stays in Vegas." Women are sometimes catty, and men can be just as bad. Work was work, although one would have to be blind not to see what had blossomed. He often left small surprises on my desk, and I did the same for him. It was normal for him to always be at my apartment. He did not feel right asking me to drive to his place. He was that guy who gave me his jacket, opened doors, pulled out chairs, watched his language, and walked on a certain side of the street. He felt that if he wanted to see me then, he should make the effort—not me. Carter was the same age as I was, but he possessed old-school chivalry…and I loved it. Life at work changed. I was relaxed with our relationship, but I still got those whispers and funny looks from a few females. When Carter and I switched cars, my coworkers were furious.

"He let her drive his car! What they got goin' on?" they asked one another.

In my mind, they could never hold a candle to me, and I wasn't about to give any thought to some average-looking females who had obviously tried to get with him and failed. They tried everything to reveal our inside bet. One chick even walked past me, wearing his jacket. She stole it from his chair, and when he realized she had it, he suggested maybe she had money issues and let her keep it. She had to explain to everyone that she wasn't broke and could buy her own jacket if she wanted to.

I got used to such episodes. I didn't talk much at work or get caught up in gossip, so it wasn't a big deal to me. During my workdays I talked to my office neighbors sometimes, and Carter and I went back and forth to each other's desks at times. I did my work, and then I went home.

Surprisingly he didn't do midnight creeps. He believed a decent woman deserved to be seen at a decent hour. However, it came to a point when neither of us wanted to say good night, so he stayed with me frequently. The majority of our time, even at my home, was spent talking. Our chat sessions involved how we grew up, where we were spiritually and financially, and our past dating horror stories. Carter was a dream man. How could I have ever said he wasn't my type? The longer I knew him, the more he disproved my first thoughts about him.

"I have waited a long time to be with someone like you, but I didn't know what to say," he confessed. "I don't share my feelings often, especially with a coworker, so you know you are quite special. Plus I just don't like rejection."

On Sundays we always got on the phone to share what we had taken from the pastor's message. Hearing a man talk that much about God and know the word did something to my heart and mind, even if I wasn't all that churchy. It made me adore him even more. And unlike Trey, Carter had no problem repeatedly telling me he loved me and exploring future possibilities with me. In many ways we were alike, sharing the same views on various topics. Some may say that would be boring, but it worked for us. I felt certain we were made for each other and that the odds were in my favor.

The atmosphere was sweeter when he was around, calm and inviting. I don't recall many outings, except for a few movie dates, but we did so many activities together at home that it didn't matter. Whenever I was sick, he made sure I did not lift a finger. I rarely had to ask for his help, since he always volunteered as if there was no other option. That was the kind of guy he was— Self-Starter Carter. He thought of anything I might need and took care of it.

"My mom is a great woman," he told me. "I watched her do everything to make sure I was straight, ya know? Food, nice clothes, a clean house…and as I got older, I loved repaying the favor in any way. That's why I take pride in helping people who help themselves, especially women. I know it isn't easy for you, so I want to do nice things for you. I know you can take care of yourself, but for some reason I don't think you have been given what you deserve. It pleases me to serve you, Miss Jasmine."

"What planet are you from, and have they started cloning yet?" I joked.

"You're different. I'm drawn to that. You have goals, and you don't beg. You're fine as wine and petite with pretty feet. You can cook, and you love the Lord. Come on, somebody. Amen!" He sounded like a bootleg preacher.

"You're crazy! I can't say I was drawn to you. I thought you were too uppity."

He bucked his eyes as if he were shocked, and then he laughed, winked at me, and said, "I'm used to hearing that. I love proving people wrong."

I recall one night when we were sitting outside on my apartment balcony. We were under a blanket on my beach chairs, watching the stars. It was his idea. The whole concept was something new to me. I always wanted to have those small sweet moments. It just didn't happen until he came along.

Our relationship was lovey-dovey indeed, but at some point I questioned why we rarely went out on dates. Whenever we did go to the movies, we always split the check. I admit I was less than enthused when that happened, but I thought God was testing me to see if I was willing to pay my own way at times. I failed that test, because it didn't take long for me to resort back to preferring chill time with him at home. When we went on dates, it felt like I was paying to be with him, and I could do that for free. Maybe this is why he liked being at home so much instead on going out. I had finally came cross a flaw. That negro was cheap! All that talk about money and attainment was making him frugal but he was the man. As for dates, *Men pay... period.*

I really didn't notice that I was seeing less and less of him outside of the office. He was great at his job but he was getting swamped with work. We still talked regularly, and when he had time, he was with me. After thinking it was just a rough patch all relationships go through, he wrote me a note at work to request that we go away for the weekend. It said, "Gotta stay late tonight but I will pick you up around 9:00 p.m. You know what to bring." That was code for lingerie and red pumps.

We headed to the nearby Hard Rock casino but for some reason, out of nowhere it stormed. I mean the clouds were dark and low and nowhere on the news did it say it would be that bad. Because of the severe weather threats of flooding, we only had dinner at the buffet and had to cut the trip short. I had literally eaten all I could and slept while he drove home. When we arrived safely to my home he walked me to my door, and he didn't come in. His blazer was wet from holding it over my head earlier in that unexpected rain. He had a serious look on his face as if he had been retaining some words for too long, and after staring off to the side, he finally spoke.

"You know I love you. I think you are so beautiful, intelligent, and..."

I stopped listening. My thoughts were all over the place trying to prepare myself for what he was going to say. *Is he proposing? Is he moving? Is he mad? Am I about to meet his momma? If he wants a baby by me, the devil is a lie!*

I stood in silence and nodded.

He continued, "I have been convicted. I feel so bad, serving God and being intimate with you—playing house. There is no right way to say this, but I've been dating you and another young lady from the church. I've basically been trying to see which of you I see a future with. I chose her."

What? All I saw was red and my blood was boiling. He went on with his "It's not you; it's me" Easter Sunday speech. Excuse after excuse came, each contradicting the next. To sum it up, I was the exciting one, the sexy one, the stimulating one, the ambitious one…but she was a younger, "plain Jane," boring, seen-but-not-heard type of female who could easily be molded and taken home to Momma. My heart plummeted and my jaw had dropped slightly but I wasn't about to cry, curse, or slap him like I wanted to. I didn't know how long he had been dating us both, but even after he had supposedly made his decision, it was not his last time being with me. All the Jesus in me seemed to disappear and I had the deepest urge to be evil. I was sick of losing after getting my hopes up with these guys. I knew he would not be able to just cease and desist. I made sure he technically cheated on her with me. I slept with him again out of spite for the both of them. I wanted him to sit at this machine and keep playing until his conscience tore him apart. Even though he stayed with her, I wanted him to question his decision for the rest of his life. Even as a young girl, I knew how to embed myself into someone's thoughts. I knew what to say and do to be carved in another's mind or heart. But lately it seemed my luck had run out. He had me thinking I was perfect for him. I thought I was the sexiest thing he'd ever seen, captivating and intelligent. *That's what all his notes said.* I actually thought I had found two guys in one with Carter, while all along this church-going cheater had doubled up with two women. Just that fast, I lost my faith and my integrity.

CHAPTER 4

QUICK PICK

*(Automatic combination generator of random numbers
for lottery games)*

I should have been down to the felt, but I still wasn't convinced all guys were bad. I knew that if I was good enough to marry Will, the other guys had simply lost out. There was no reason to beat myself up about guys who obviously had no sense and would probably make me miserable in the long run anyway. So maybe I'd dodged a couple of bullets. I still had male friends, so I went on dates and had fun. I was *not* sitting at home, being bitter and feeling down. I began to wonder why I even wanted a relationship. What I really needed was to take a break and focus on myself, but I got bored and found myself in the company of a new love interest. I wasn't letting myself get all excited about *anyone*. I decided to play by my own rules for a while and deal the cards. If guys wanted to spend time and money on me, I was game but only when *I* felt like it. It wasn't really about what they wanted but more so about what *I* wanted. Even if I was bored out of my mind, I hesitated to ask a guy out. On the inside I was bruised, not broken, but nobody needed to know that. I wanted to prove that I felt fine. It got to be that I could predict when certain guys would call. I kicked back and enjoyed my random picks. I didn't talk to guys on the phone much, because I didn't want to get attached. I still wanted to spend most of my time at home. I was usually in a T-shirt and pajama pants with my hair in a ponytail, watching Lifetime TV or my favorite DVD—*Love Jones*, when most of the people around me assumed I was having the time of my life partying with friends or on dates with hot guys. All that hibernating only encouraged guys to ask me out more and try even harder to hang out or kick it with me. I wasn't trying to be serious with anyone, but then I realized I wasn't OK with bouncing around with different faces. It was in my nature to have consistency and stability with one person. It was also in my nature to always have male companions. I had no idea what to do. I was struggling to keep up, going 'round and 'round in this losing circle. I had made it a cycle. I was still looking good and dressing sexy for the few dates I accepted. I kept my emotional guard up, because I knew either I would get tired of the guys or they would just fade away. It became as natural as the change of seasons for a guy's time to be up, and he went into the discard tray. I kept my demeanor so easygoing and pleasant that I didn't know why I didn't just meet "the one." I juggled scary thoughts of marrying at a very old age, never marrying at all, marrying someone on a whim, or get married to a man to secretly had someone else. That's when I noticed my bad attitude for women. It wasn't enough that I hurt the guys who hurt me, but I had to have malice in my heart for whomever the guys chose to love. I knew I wanted marriage only once, so it had to be based on more than just physical attraction, insecurity and a few fun times. I needed to be with someone I could love unconditionally every day for the rest of my life. For me to have that, he would have to be a true friend first. I thought I knew what that meant. I'd had male friends before. During all my ups and downs, I had Devin. All through my college years and beyond, he stood out to me in a different way. He was the only one called me Jazz, and I could tell him how stupid all the guys in my past were while he laughed it off with me. Hanging out with him was like being with a relative or one of my girlfriends. He told me hilarious stories about his "tramps," as he called them. At first I didn't see how he could have had so many women. He looked all right, but not somebody I could see myself with. He was actually really sweet and loved to laugh. He always used sarcasm and humor to help me forgot whatever bothered me. One night I finally took him up on his offer to hang out with him and his grandma at Bingo and later of course, out to eat.

"If you weren't so damn greedy, maybe guys would keep you around," he joked.

"What?"

"Girl, you eat too much."

"But you keep taking me out and feeding me. It must not be a problem on my end."

"I just do it 'cause you're so ugly, Jazz. It's charity."

"Whatever, Devin!"

He cut me no slack, and when I caught on to his ways I threw jabs right back. I figured he probably had a crush on me, but he never once said anything to even remotely indicate that. I was so relieved. If I knew what having a male best friend was, he fit the description. But one thing I didn't know about him was where he worked. All he would do was say I was nosey and that all I needed to know was he got the job done. So I called him a janitor. He was acting just like Tommy from the show Martin, never revealing where he worked. *You ain't got no job, man,* I thought to myself. I often wondered how long it would be before he tried to come on to me. I had agreed to spend the night with him once to watch stand-up comedy movies, and before I arrived he gave me call.

"Jazz, please bring some decent pajamas, not that raggedy bullshit ya'll women wear around the house."

I fell out laughing. "Why are you worried about what I'll have on? Do you want to buy me some pajamas?"

"Negative. I ain't your man. And no, you can't sleep in my shirts. You're too old for that shit."

He was never serious in what he said. He was just a jokester, who laughed at himself as much as I did. If I didn't know how much he watched Martin Lawrence, Eddie Murphy, Richard Pryor or Chris Rock, we probably wouldn't have been friends because his language was filthy. I just knew he meant nothing by it.

I stayed at his house often, and he never tried to kiss, hug, or touch me. I was confused yet so impressed that I started to like him...a lot. Of course, I never said anything because I didn't want to mess up our friendship. He bought me whatever I wanted and it seemed a little odd that I was getting so much from him, and he wanted nothing in return. He was still just as silly and sarcastic as ever. The fun I had with him reminded me of Trey, but it was different. For one Trey didn't swear around me. Devin and I always hung out at Bingo and a local small casino. It wasn't a spectacular sight to see but it had enough business to stay open. He gave me money to play, otherwise I would have been content with the free drinks and listening to his Granny swear all night. She was a cute, feisty little woman born on February 14. When Devin told me his grandmother's birthday I just smiled and nodded like I always do when I'm speechless. *You gotta be kidding me. Granny is a lot of things but a valentine doesn't strike me as one of 'em.* He once took me on a trip out of state and still didn't try anything. We were just friends, and I knew he had a girlfriend along with a few more on the side. I guessed in his twisted mind he was being faithful, but where was his girlfriend when he was with me? I didn't see Devin *all* the time, but when I did, I knew to pack clothes. I think the reason I didn't see him as more than a friend was because I'd heard the stories of all his women. I often told him his penis was going to rot off if he didn't sit down somewhere. His life reminded me of the casino slogan "Where girls go to play."

I never judged him, but I told him to be careful. As a friend, I cared about his well-being. I loved him, but I was not in love. He was my buddy. We swapped stories about our lives, watched movies, ate, and slept. He was almost like an annoying cousin I loved being around. I remember the night I had him to pick me up because the weather was terrible and the power was out in my apartment. He was ready with the jokes.

"I guess your lights really were off… but the water too?"

"Shut the hell up, Devin. I'm using your water tonight. Did your tramp pay the bill?"

"Please brush your teeth before you talk to me in the morning."

"Devin, you need to brush yours now. *Your* breath is what's keeping me up."

"Good night, ugly," we said in unison.

I turned over in my pajamas and was almost in a deep sleep before he spoke again. "If you snore or pass gas, you will wake up on the streets where you came from."

I laughed so hard I had tears coming out of my eyes. He had to have the last word, but I always had him beat. "Lord, thank you for my friend Devin. Please don't punish him if he doesn't close his eyes during this prayer. They are too big, and he just can't close 'em. Fix it, Jesus. Amen."

A soft pillow frequently swept across my head, but I was laughing too hard care.

One year around my birthday, I was bored at home and did not expect anything because I was still single. I was hoping I would get my usual Happy Birthday text that morning from Trey but I walked away from my phone with tears in my eyes when I didn't. *I gotta stop expecting to hear from him.* A few hours later my phone rang. *Trey?*

"Hey, ugly, put some clothes on and come downstairs. I'll be waiting."

"Huh? Devin, I'm in the bed. What are you talking about?"

"I know. I smell your breath through the phone. Borrow some soap from a friend, put some clothes on, and come downstairs, woman!"

I said I would come down but I wasn't even smiling because I was still disappointed at Trey. *He really forgot my birthday! I can't believe this. What kinda chic is he with that he can't even tell me happy birthday. That heffa...* I was sitting there just fussing in my mind when my phone started ringing. I thought it was Trey but all I heard was Devin as soon as I answered.

"Jazz. Does it take that long? Hell ya lil' funky birthday will be over by the time..."

"I'm coming fool!" I interrupted, "I was giving you some time to put some gum in your mouth."

Devin was working my nerves, but I was still excited to get out of that apartment. At least somebody thought about me. *Where is his girlfriend? Is he really going to wait for me, not knowing how long I will be?* He did. He greeted me with flowers, candy, and a gift that I was told not to open until I got back home. It was the best birthday I could remember. We had food and drinks, went to a movie, and headed to the casino to listen to some live music. When I returned home from a night of laughter and fun, I opened my gift. It was a beautiful red and black chiffon lingerie set from Victoria's Secret. It was classy, trimmed in silk, embroidered, and expensive. I knew because he'd left the hundred-dollar price tag on it. I'd never told him my size, but it was exactly right. I later asked what inspired him to get me such a gift.

"I'll never see it on you, but I knew you'd think it was pretty. Don't wear this for none of your freaky boyfriends. Just wear it for yourself. You can't be a slut all ya life."

I smacked the crap out of him and laughed. "Thank you. I don't get you sometimes, but that's because you're a little slow."

He laughed and shook his head. "Happy birthday though, for real," he said, driving off.

Devin was like the boys in my kindergarten class. If they liked me, they pulled my hair or tied my shoelaces together to see if I'd trip. I really liked him. I wanted to wash his mouth out with soap and knock him out sometimes, but I liked him.

Devin had no hidden agenda or ulterior motives, so I felt safe around him. I didn't have to wager, bet, or take risks. I knew exactly who he was, and he didn't put on a front for me. I trusted him only as a friend, and I vowed to myself that I would never jeopardize that with intimacy. I was very serious about that decision, and I stuck to it. Because of this, our friendship never died. The question did come up at some point about whether we should try being more than friends, but I couldn't do it. I wanted to but couldn't. As a boyfriend, I didn't trust him at all, because I knew he had a lot of women and a primary girlfriend he was cheating on. Would he have given them up for me? Would I have given up my old trusties for him? I will never know. I let it ride as long as I could, until he married his longtime girlfriend. But we remained associates. I rarely saw him face-to-face after that. He respected me, and I appreciated him. I was happy with the way things turned out as strictly friends. But I would miss being myself with him and knowing he was always there for me to vent, be pampered, and laugh the night away. I'm glad we never crossed the line in our friendship, but I still lost my comfort and my joy.

CHAPTER 5

SNAKE EYES

(Rolling a two in craps—"eyes" because the dots look like eyes and "snake" because they are bad news)

I enjoyed being single for good while after Devin got married, because I finally understood that companionship was more important than random dating. Being focused during my single time, I purchased my first home and completed my master's degree. I still partied with my friends and went out with guys occasionally, and for the most part, I was content. A friend convinced me to create a social media page to reconnect with old classmates and relatives. For about a year, I spent hours finding former friends, posting pictures and songs, and communicating with all types of people. As I scrolled through some pictures of people I knew, I kept noticing a handsome unfamiliar face. He and I had mutual colleagues. I honestly do not recall who made the first attempt at a conversation, but I remember it was in April because our birthdays were one week apart. When running across pictures on social media, we posted random comments about each other, such as, *who's the handsome guy in the blue shirt*? Or, *who's the pretty girl in the jeans*? He asked me out after we had flirted to the extreme online. I agreed and was back on path to being wined and dined. I still wasn't trying to be serious with anyone, but his face and smile took me to another world. His eyelashes went on for days, and his slim body was so inviting. Looking at him was like finding a miracle in the desert. During our first date, I probably heard only four of his sentences all night. His lips were so perfect and full that I wanted to run my fingers across them while he was talking. This guy was very attractive and charming. Yet somehow, straightforward and arrogant at the same time. This pretty boy was self-aware and knew what he wanted in life. I had an eerie feeling that he asked me questions for his own agenda, not because he cared about my answers. I was tipping the dealer, without knowing it. His name was Anthony.

"So tell me one of your pet peeves," he said.

"Liars. People get caught up in saying what they think people want to hear, but the truth is so much better."

"I agree one hundred percent. People should just be honest. OK, my next question is…what should I know about you, sweetheart?"

"I'm addictive," I said, smiling.

His teeth were perfect, practically flashing a sparkle like in a Colgate commercial. He leaned in, looked straight at me, bit that juicy bottom lip of his, and whispered, "So am I."

For several months we enjoyed movies, great food, music, dancing…liquor, wine, and beer. Or should I have just said "alcohol"? I'd never been much of a drinker, but I trusted him since he gave me no sign that he was irresponsible. We always safely made it to our destinations, and no matter how much he drank, he was always sweet and affectionate. He drank a lot, and pretty soon, so did I. I actually had to put a wine rack in my house because I had so many bottles of different wines and liquors. Empty bottles lined my kitchen counters. I saved them because of how cute the bottles were and as reminders of what I had tasted. I loved Nuvo bottles, which resembled perfume decanters. Most people save things that might bring them luck, such as a four-leaf clover, rabbit's foot, or lucky dice, but I had a houseful of empty liquor bottles. Hey, they'd brought me a new man so I collected them like trophies. In a short time, I met his parents, siblings, and grandparents. I was very comfortable with him. We didn't spend every moment together, but when we went out, we always looked like a million bucks. We enjoyed seeing each other at parties, flirting all night as if we were strangers, and then leaving to spend the rest of our evening snuggled up in his tidy, perfectly organized apartment. It was almost *too* clean. His bathroom was worthy of a home-interior magazine spread, complete with monogrammed towels and a teeth-whitening kit on the sink. Never was even one dish in the sink. Vacuum lines scored the carpet. And of course, beautiful wine glasses were waiting on the two of us.

I enjoyed Anthony very much. He had a sense of humor underneath his refinement. He almost reminded me of Carter but taller and with a light caramel complexion. Or was it honey? He wasn't dark or high yellow. He was a prefect shade of brown, with wavy jet-black hair and those long eyelashes. Anthony and I talked on the phone a lot, and he texted me several times throughout each day with smiley faces and sweet messages: *I miss you*, *Where are you?* And then *I love you.* Our relationship moved pretty quickly, but I didn't mind at all. He had a great job as a realtor, he was sweet, he loved his family, and most of all, and he loved me. I had never been called "sweetheart" so much until I met him.

"Do you have any diamonds, Jasmine?" he asked one day.

"I have a necklace and a ring, but that's all."

My birthstone is the diamond. I've always loved jewels, but Will was the only guy to ever give me diamonds.

"Well, sweetheart, I have to get you some diamond earrings. What else do you like?"

"I like the gifts women think they have outgrown, like stuffed animals, cards, candy, love notes, and flowers just because."

"Oh, OK, I see. You're a girlie girl, huh?" He smiled. "That's no problem, sweetheart."

In the course of our relationship, I should have asked several questions about his past. But he was always with me and very affectionate even in public, so I didn't worry about it. I was too focused on the moment. Out of all the guys in my past, I thought he was the finest with the biggest, prettiest smile. That teeth whitener he always used must've paid off, since I always saw the sparkle when he smiled. I liked this cocky guy, and as fine as he was, his eyes never roamed. He was too hooked on me, and I loved it. He always looked at me like he was two seconds away from tearing off my clothes and throwing me over his shoulder like a caveman. He knew how to have a good time but he always had a cup or glass of liquor. I wasn't used to that much drinking, but I ignored it because Anthony kept me on a high some women dream about. I could have used social media as a way to dig up information or at least scroll through more pictures. But I thought, *why would I do that, when his pretty self is in my face, in my arms, in my bed, and most of all, in my head?* And he had money to spend on me! This high roller was all over me. True enough, he was sort of new to me, but I didn't feel like checking to see who or what was in his past. Anthony was an on-a-need-to-know-basis type guy. He didn't bring up anything old, and didn't ask me about my past.

He explained, "Sometimes we ask questions we really don't want answered."

"True."

"Right. Then anytime an issue comes up, we go straight to whatever old stories we heard and replay it over and over." he continued.

"Sometimes, though, old stories help you know more about a person."

"It can't stop people from telling you what they want you to know at that time. It just creates the blame game. Even if my past were squeaky clean, it doesn't mean I'm not capable of being a bad guy, right?"

"I see. And if you had a terrible past, it doesn't mean you can't change and turn out great." I replied, seeing that he wasn't giving up any information.

"Exactly."

Quite often I had to calm him down after his many family feuds. Some family member always called to tell him bad news.

He was the family mediator, and—it didn't matter where we were—when he was needed, he flew out the door to try to stop some madness from going on.

He often said, "I gotta go break up this fight, sweetheart. My folks are crazy," or, "So-and-so pulled out a gun and is threatening to shoot everybody." I was with him many times when his phone rang, and sure enough, a relative, friend, or someone's baby mama was calling him because "cousin Skeet done snapped" or "Pookie jumped on Ray-Ray" or "LaQuisha is fighting drunk." Alright, I'm exaggerating a bit but for as classy as he was, he knew some mighty ratchet people. I wondered how it was that he was so normal while everybody close to him was psycho.

We finally sat down and talked, and he revealed some not-so-great memories and issues he was still trying to work through. Even though he lived alone, he was very much involved with his family, and I admired that. His was a broken family, with several different battles going on, and they all called on him to set situations right. He always came straight back to me if he had to leave to settle an argument, and it felt nice that he confided in me. I felt like I was his breath of fresh air, his comforter…but nothing consoled him like alcohol. Many nights when things got crazy with his family, we talked about it and drank. I don't know why I drank so much, but I almost felt like I had to so we could be on one accord. The alcohol turned us into people who had no fear, no shame, and no hurt. But I put too much of myself on the table with Anthony, playing this game like a pigeon. We never went to church together. Several Sundays I missed going on my own because I woke up hung over. Pretty soon the truth unfolded. He pulled some disappearing acts, claiming he had so many family issues that he needed to be alone. He said he didn't want to bring sadness to me. For months we had been inseparable, and then out of nowhere he was picking arguments and saying he needed space. Then I heard rumors that he was seeing other women. I spotted new comments, smiley faces, and hearts on his social media photos. When I asked about the females I saw posting things on his page, he said he didn't know who they were.

"Sweetheart, I guess they just found my pictures the same way you did. I can't stop them from posting. In case you haven't noticed, I don't reply."

"You might not reply, but if you post a picture of you with me, I wonder what your little fan club would say."

He laughed. "You got jokes, huh? Girl, you know the whole world is on these sites. I see it, but I ignore it. I'm with you—where I wanna be."

His way of showing me how he felt about me—or maybe of shutting me up—was always with sex and alcohol. I surrendered to his gaming system every time.

He would grab my hair, lick the side of my face, and say, "Let's get drunk." I didn't mind the grabbing and licking part, but the problem was that he was already drunk.

I did not hear from him for weeks at a time. Sometimes a month went by. I scrolled through his profile pictures and comments, tracing pictures of him out dining or just chilling with other females. In the photos, his eyes were always red, and the young ladies were somewhat attractive. They weren't as fine as I was, but I could see how alcohol might make them desirable.

I was pissed. I called him and texted him but got no response. Out of the blue, he texted, *I miss you.* I was livid and confused. He didn't know I had seen the photos of the other females. I was rolling dice, not knowing how they would land. He sometimes saw me out socializing and apologized, especially if other guys were talking to me. Other times he just called as if nothing had happened. A few times he just showed up at my house.

"What are you doing?" I asked. "You say you miss me but then vanish for no reason. You don't even tell me why. Why are you here?"

"I know. I had so much going on, and I didn't want to keep putting my issues on you. I was trying to give you space."

"I didn't ask for space—you did! I don't live with you. My house *is* my space. You're full of shit, and you know it!"

"Please don't think that. Just come over later, and talk to me. I'll explain everything. I miss you and love you, sweetheart. Don't do me like that. I'll leave my door open and wait on you."

And he did. Several times we had that same conversation, and I walked through that door of his every time. My favorite movie or music might be playing, and I had blankets, wine, and him. He talked, with tears in his eyes, about the confusion he dealt with all the time. I knew he was hiding something big, but with the way he apologized...oh my goodness, I didn't stand a chance.

But each time he disappeared, it became more and more dramatic. Pretty soon we were arguing on a regular basis, and I was not used to that. He mentioned that maybe we needed to see other people since we weren't getting along. I thought, *Nigga, you're already seeing other people!* But I didn't say that, because I knew he would deny it. He always said the other women were just friends or meant nothing to him. The truth was—I didn't mean anything to him either. I never remembered how the arguments started, but I didn't back down from them. It became almost normal to be in turmoil, yet somehow we knew it wasn't over yet. Anthony played the game hard, using sex to grease my palms. I had to break down and start asking questions. My cousin, who had gone to high school with him, gave me an earful.

"How in the world did you end up with him?" My cousin laughed.

"What are you talkin' about? This just happened out of nowhere. Is he crazy?"

"Ha-ha…yep, and pretty soon you will be too."

"Hold on, hold on, hold on! How am *I* going to be crazy?"

"Let me explain, lil' cousin. He's always been like this. He was lame in school, but he got older and prettier, and the girls who once ignored him, started going after him."

"Oh, really?"

"He ain't tryin' to be nobody's man. Some girl dumped him when he was younger, and he ain't been right since. He ain't gonna hurt you, but he will mess your mind up. This is his routine: ya'll gonna go out, ya'll gonna stay drunk, he's gonna screw the shit outta you, he's gonna cheat on you, he'll lie about it, and then he'll vanish with no warning. He breaks up with the best-looking, smartest girls he can and leaves them no closure. Man, I can't believe you made it with him over a month."

It had been a year. We were just like Jody and Yvette in the film *Baby Boy*, fussing about whether he was seeing other females. Fortunately our arguments were never physical. Anthony wasn't a mean guy, but he was a liar—exactly what I'd told him I didn't like. He had a need for commotion, which made him want intense makeup sex. Between the alcohol and confusion, I gave him what he was already accustomed to— more commotion. I didn't know if I was coming or going with him. We were together, then apart, and together again. If we were at the same party or event, even if we hadn't spoken in a long time, we left together. We could not stay apart. I stayed because I was trying to prove I wasn't like the ladies from his past. I hoped he would tire of the episodes and just trust me. I doubled up on my bet that he wasn't going to leave me or wring me out emotionally. If he acted a certain way, I behaved the same way…times ten. I was trying to wear him out so he would throw in his cards. He never broke down.

When we decided to start over, he let his guard down. That was the beginning of the end. He stopping hiding his phone and turning his ringer off, and I gave him no reason to feel he had to. Everything was calm for a short moment. A few times he mistakenly sent me text messages meant for other females. More females posted pictures *of* him and *with* him on social media pages. His explanation for the texts was that other people were using his phone. As for the pictures, he claimed those girls were just friends he hung out with and not dates.

"I don't even know why that girl waited until now to post that picture. It's so old."

"Oh, so I guess because you are taken, now all your friends want to post old pictures and get you in trouble, huh?"

"Yep, that's so childish. I didn't know people were hating on us like that."

"We'll see."

"So anyway, sweetheart, what do you want for Valentine's Day?"

"Surprise me."

February 14 fell on a Thursday, and I wasn't very excited about it since I had to work during the day and he had to work that night. But I knew I was in for a passionate weekend. I sat at my desk, and coworkers were called over the intercom one by one to come to the lobby. They came back with gifts, balloons, fruit bouquets, roses, and candy. I never heard my name. I couldn't wait to get away from all that Valentine's stuff, but I wished I had gotten a gift at work. I talked to Anthony, and he said he wished he didn't have to work but that he would make it up to me. I got off the phone with him and went home. I stepped into my bedroom, and gifts were all over my bed along with an adorable life-sized teddy bear. I could not believe it. It was like scratching off a lottery ticket and seeing all my numbers. I didn't recall giving him a key, but I didn't care because I had presents. It had been a while since I had actually scored anything. A long time ago, he'd asked me what I liked and I told him—and he'd gotten it all. He worked overnight, so when he got off work the next day, I was asleep and probably still smiling. He invited me back to his apartment. I walked in and heard low jazz music. I was led to his room, where the bed was dressed in black satin sheets and red candles flickered. A balcony was connected, and the doors were wide open. We heated up pretty quickly that weekend, and for two days and nights, we slid from those satin sheets to the balcony and back. His neighbors likely heard us since we took it outside. Every time the moonlight hit his face, I thought, *dang, he really is that fine*. I'm sure we were drunk, but it was the freakiest, stickiest, sweatiest, craziest sex I'd ever had. *Whew!* Part of me hated myself for it, and part of me was just too wrapped up in the pleasure to even imagine letting it go.

As usual extreme highs were followed by extreme lows, and this time was no different. A few months had passed when I found out he never showed for work on February 14. He instead went on a date with another woman and took her back to his house, where he presented her with all the same gifts he had bought me. What Anthony and I did for a full weekend, he and that chick did in one night. I wanted to run him over! I bleached all his clothes, threw his things into the street, and torched the gifts. Yes, I set a big-ass teddy bear on fire. Of course, Anthony lied. He said he had gone to work and that the girl popped up at his apartment earlier in the day. He said the gifts she claimed were hers were the ones he hadn't brought to my house yet.

"I didn't buy that crazy ho a thing. Those were your gifts. She assumed they were hers. I made her leave, and I brought them to your house while you were gone. I was at work! I called you when I got off work. Come off that nonsense!" he shouted.

I noticed that every lie he told rolled off his tongue like honey, and he kept a straight face. I thought about how I used to act mad at Will but really didn't care. I just played the game so we could eventually break up. Yeah, it was the same move. I knew that move—I created that move. Ironically, Anthony had just done the same thing to me.

Suddenly his lies made perfect sense. I had ignored the deception because I was too far gone in the chaotic ritual we had created. Of course I didn't hear from him for a while. More pictures went up of him with his "friends," and I became a drama queen. I didn't like any girl who even looked twice at him. Eventually Anthony came back around and admitted he was seeing other girls—but only during times when he and I were not talking, or so he said. When I realized how many different girls there were, I was furious and compared myself. *Is my skin too light...too dark? Am I too independent? Should I go natural, keep my perm, or get a weave? Is my booty not big enough? Do I have love handles? I know it isn't my boobs. What do they have that I don't? Why can't a guy just to be with me? What the hell is wrong with me?* I was so confused, and I had never questioned or doubted myself in such a way before. I was using him as a measuring tool for my own worth. But how could I measure myself with a broken ruler? He was no good when we met, and mentally he couldn't have been playing with a full deck of cards.

I still wasn't ready to tap out, determined to go another round. I wanted to get him hooked on me like never before and then drop him. I dressed sexier, and I went on dates with cute guys I really had no interest in. I purposely visited places where I knew he would be and walked by as if he didn't exist. I didn't realize this placed me in a category with every other regular female. Nothing about me was special, classy, or mysterious. I thought jealousy would make him realize what he had, and then I could stop acting and looking like a tramp. I saw a million text messages from him, and I ignored them all. I loved it. He was jealous and territorial, just like I wanted. But who knew how exhausting it would be? Anthony wasn't in love with me—he loved chaos. I finally gave up on a serious relationship with him, but I still wanted to fool around. I loved him at one time, but he called, texted, or popped up at my house, *not* to show he cared but to make sure I had no time for anyone else. He kept a wall between us. He didn't fully trust any woman. He just knew how to please us. I felt too invested in him to cut it off, and I kept thinking things would settle down. We had instant chemistry every time we collided, and our arguments were not serious. They were just excuses for him to date other people. He loved the company of women but did not value one over the next. I met him at a time when he was telling ladies what they wanted to hear.

Anthony tried one last time to get back with me, following me around a party. He asked friends why I was being so mean to him. He was trying to make me laugh, but I was so through with him. I still had love in me but not for him. I talked to him one last time, when he denied having a baby on the way. Everyone has lied before, but for a man to deny his own child was despicable. If Anthony had a dollar for each lie he told, he'd have a true jackpot instead of being a real jackass. I don't know why I dealt with the foolishness for so long, but the person I had become was unfamiliar. This new person was jealous, insecure, and suspicious. I went through his phone and always saw what I wished I never had. I'd resorted to vandalism, yelling, and throwing things. For two years all I did with this guy was drink, go to clubs, argue, and screw. Going to church when I did go was pointless. I almost felt that if I sat on a church pew, it might go up in flames. I lost my dignity, and like my cousin predicted, I had lost my damn mind.

CHAPTER 6

COLD STREAK

(An extended losing run)

Before things faded completely with Anthony, I was already meeting new people and conversing on the phone or through the Internet as I had done before. Of course, I had no intentions of becoming serious with anyone, but I also didn't plan to be bored and dateless. I was a total mess. I had gone to extremes with so many different guys, and I always ended up empty-handed. Friendships were gone. Dates and gifts were gone. Sex—that was damn near perfect —was gone. I really thought I was a lost cause, but I gave guys chance after chance, just to lose myself slowly but surely.

I had ruined almost every friendship with my home girls just by being in denial when they tried to talk to me about my dating foolishness. I wasn't there for them like I should have been, and I was offended by everything anyone said to help about me. I used that as an excuse to not only bad-mouth them but cut them off completely. They cared about me but I had been angry for long that I lashed out-at my long-time friend, Ashley. Ashley spoke her mind and didn't care about hurting my feelings.

"See that's the problem, Jay. You think what looks good *is* good." she said.

"Not true. I can't help that I get the kinda guys that you can't. Even the preacher said *we what attract what we are*. And I know I'm cute." I said jokingly.

"Really? Cute is an opinion but crazy is a sure thing!"

"When you stop taking your lonely self to movies, discover some MAC, and stop borrowing my clothes I'll listen to you."

"Oh hell no, *you* stop borrowing men. From what I see they all belong to someone else."

"Oh, you mean like the nigga that left you and married a white girl? Don't go there."

"You know what, I learned my lesson. Everything that glitters ain't gold!", and she slammed the phone down. The love escapades with those men were ruining my life like poison. Admittedly I had turned into a total bitch. I wasn't proud of myself as a young lady, sister, daughter, or friend but no way was I was going to church. I tried before, and it seemed every sermon was directed at me negatively. I wanted to be uplifted, not singled out. My mind played tricks on me, as if everyone I met was going to be in my life to take something and then leave. Even though I talked to guys on the phone, I think I hated all men for a moment. And I hated who I had become. I went through spells when I stopped answering phone calls or going out. Many times I even caught myself driving and looking over into trenches and rivers, wanting to drive off. I had gone into a dark place, but I never let it show. When I was on the phone, I listened to other people's problems and told them they would be all right. I was doing what I had learned—telling people what they wanted to hear.

I stayed to myself because I felt so hurt by men that I knew I would hurt someone else badly if I had the chance. If I had to endure one more heartache, I was ready to kill somebody. I was like a female version of Dr. Jekyll and Mr. Hyde. One day I was fine, the next a ticking time bomb. I didn't understand how I'd gone from being one person's queen of hearts to dealing with a bunch of jokers. I was spiraling downhill, and it seemed like happiness ran from me. I just wanted a man to be as great as he'd presented himself in the beginning. Thinking back to the past, I knew I could not have forced myself to marry Will. I was not in love, but at least I knew he was in love with me. I didn't think that type of love would come around again. At this point, I felt I didn't even deserve it.

My relationships were a complete mess. I was never hurt enough to try romancing women, but I was hurt enough to basically date totally out of my character: guys that were too young, married, too old, dope dealers, and even in gangs. Since I believed all men were liars, I figured they might as well be handsome and fun to be around. I didn't even care if they had money or not. I just wanted their time and for them to be cute. I didn't consider men as valuable, reliable, or even intelligent creatures. Dating guys had become a hobby. It was what I did when I was bored, and I was good at it. It kept me busy. I didn't express that I wanted true love, so it was even harder for me to find it. I had dimmed my own shine so much that I was convinced love certainly couldn't find me.

Ultimately I trained myself to believe true love was a waste of time and a myth. It felt like I had been sitting at a slot machine for years, and instead of getting a few coins back, I got nothing. I thought about the questions that went through my mind as a young girl in the casino with my mom. *How could people gamble away their rent money, a whole paycheck, or their entire life savings? Did the same people who seemed to win in casinos end up losing their cars and homes?* I was just like them. Over and over, I thought having a new man in my life was surely going to lead me to the perfect romance. *You know, like a happily-ever-after story.* Hope was one thing, but wishful thinking was another. I didn't have either. I just had problems. My inside was broken. My mind frame was in the negative. My identity had been repossessed.

I had to step back and take a look at myself. If someone were to prove he was in love with me and only me, then yes, I would be willing to try dating again. But it was not going to happen overnight, and it wasn't going to happen at all unless I carried myself like a winner. I had buried some of my most wonderful traits under a rug and was obsessed with relationships. I wanted companionship, but I wasn't even a good friend to those around me. I needed to go back and think about who I had been years ago before I started acting as if a guy's opinion determined my worth. I realized I was still great no matter who didn't see it. Blaming guys for failed relationships wasn't the answer either, because I always had a choice to leave and didn't. I stayed in situations and pushed my own feelings aside to please others and maintain a false sense of love. I needed to wise up. I could easily close my eyes and see parts of me slide across a green table into the hands of those I kept betting with. The money, coins, chips, and jewels were transformed in my mind to all the admirable traits that made me Jasmine Jones. I was empty, and I had lost my purpose. It was finally time to fold and stop gambling myself away.

CHAPTER 7

JACKPOT

(An impressive, often unexpected success or reward)

It had been a long time since I had actually paid attention to a sermon. I treated church like a casino too. I put money in the collection plate, hoping to be lifted up and hear a particular message or a certain song. I often debated on going because I wasn't sure I would enjoy myself. If it wasn't packed, the choir didn't sing my favorite songs, or Lord forbid I had to hear a guest speaker instead of our beloved pastor, then it was a waste of time for me. It was just a reason for me to dress up and disguise how I felt inside. My church attendance had dwindled down to every other Sunday, and that turned into whenever I felt like it. Since most Sundays I wasn't even waking up in my own home, I usually decided to just listen to gospel music all day. Something in me knew that wasn't enough. I had to go to church and hear a word, no matter who delivered it. I needed a distraction to take my mind away from my failed relationships. I made myself go to church because my life was on the table. I had been headed in the wrong direction for the past few years, and it seemed I had only two options: 1) I could pretend to not care anymore, being with anyone and everybody since love was a joke, lying to people that I didn't need companionship, or 2) I could just accept that I was not the winning ticket for anyone and be alone.

To my fortune, the game changed one Sunday when the pastor preached about relationships.

I knew I wasn't the only one who mistakes when it came to love. The pastor's message said that dating was not about finding perfection but gaining wisdom. The message also said that, whether we know it or not, the Lord worked on all individuals before putting them together. This did not mean both people would be the "total package" as soon as they met, but if their hearts and minds were in the right place, that was the perfect winning combination every time—and that main Powerball choice had to always be the Lord. Without spiritual guidance I would experience only a percentage of the true love and joy He wanted for my life. I realized the first relationship that needed work was my spiritual one. I decided to let go and let God. Whatever I had been doing obviously wasn't working, and I had been neglecting time with the Lord. I became all right with trusting the fact that he would send my companion when the time was right.

Instead of focusing on what guys wanted, or even what I wanted, I had to give God what he wanted. He wanted me to revisit the old me—the girl I was before college—and see why I was so delightfully spoiled. Why did guys love being around me and doing things for me back then? They weren't trying to get anything from me. I knew this because I didn't have money and sure as heck wasn't giving up any cookies back then. I was just authentically being me. I was kind, spoke my mind, had no favorites, made people laugh, was involved with the community, and visited the elderly. I got good grades in school, carried myself well, played instruments, was a great artist, could make just about anything with my hands, pushed myself to achieve goals, and genuinely cared about people. The key was that I knew how valuable I was, and I always found a way to shine and help other people do the same. But who would know all those great things, looking at the road I went down? I could not think of one guy in my adult life that really knew those attributes about me. So what had those guys been there for? What was I showing them? Being cute, smart, and funny only took me so far in the game. I was dealing with situations that called for strategy and strength. The one time I came close to having a solid relationship, I picked the guy apart and sabotaged it. Even if I didn't want to be with Will, there was a better way to handle my feelings around the relationship. My entire dating life was a game of roulette. I was the little ball being dropped onto a revolving wheel with different compartments of guys and situations, not knowing where I would land. I might not have been familiar with Lady Luck, but I surely met up with karma. Yep, she's still a bitch. But no matter how I felt about the cards life dealt and the bad moves I made, I kept trying to win time after time.

It took a little while, but I stepped away from it all and worked on building myself up. Going back to my old hobbies helped. Just telling myself how fabulous I was helped. Focusing on my career and education helped. Dressing fierce, going out by myself, and coming home alone all helped. I wasn't trying to catch anyone's eye except for God's. If I wasn't my best me, how could God send my lucky charm? Why would God go through the trouble of preparing someone just for me if I didn't care enough to willingly be prepared by God?

Life did not stop happening. Some tough times came, and I thought about how none of the guys in my past could have helped me anyway. I went through difficult moments, and sometimes I got so lonely that I tried to rekindle some old flames. But it never worked, because I had changed for the better. A divinely invisible wedge kept me from going back to my past. It was God's way of making me look straight ahead and keep going forward. As for the times when I didn't have sense enough to cut off ties with guys, God made it so they cut ties with me. Although I felt hurt sometimes, it had to happen that way for me to move ahead. I texted guys, and they did not respond—none of them. I was beautiful, young, intelligent…and single.

I wasn't always satisfied with that, but I gathered up the pieces of myself that I thought were lost and left my heart in God's hands. And I felt better. Finally I could look in the mirror and recognize myself. A long time went by, and occasionally I got so frustrated that the tears did not stop. I had to quit living in regret and wishing my life had gone differently. Had I not gone through my ups and downs, I would not have realized how important it was to know and believe God's love required more of me...as well as more *for* me. I had lowered my standards, ignored many red flags, and swapped being understanding with naïveté. There was a difference. I let so much just roll on, thinking it would right itself over time. But how can two broken people fix a relationship? A reality check reminded me that no matter how much time I spent doing wrong, it would never magically get right. It took inner work. When I realized all this, my life brightened up.

I continued to attend church, really enjoying myself, and I even helped organize the church's bingo night. I hated the idea of gambling in church but that was the easiest game I could think of. The object of the game was to have someone read a Bible verse and the players would match it with the correct scripture on their boards. The winners received Visa gift cards. During regular Sunday service, I sensed a few glances my way from a new member. I thought, *He is cute, but I don't think so.* I kept looking straight ahead. A few times we accidently ran in to each other after service and exchanged smiles. I had been single for nearly two years and had no energy for games. One Sunday morning, I began my routine of turning on the gospel radio station, taking an energizing shower, and choosing my outfit for service. I arrived to church already smiling, just because I was blessed to see another day. My 30th birthday was approaching and two years after Anthony left, I wasn't just single—I was free. I had no new faces to figure out, and nobody was trying charm me into a dead-end situation—no drama, no lies, no headaches. Nobody owed me anything, and I didn't owe anyone. My relationship gambling debts were paid in full. I was hearing from the Lord, and his messages were loud and clear.

"Excuse me, do you have a pen?" whispered a raspy voice from the church row behind me.

Without turning around, I handed one back.

"Thanks, pretty lady."

I still didn't turn around but nodded to keep from being distracted. The pastor's message was on point, and I was totally engaged in it. The choir had me in tears as angelic yet powerful voices sang "Total Praise." I seemed to be in a magical place. After the service I made my usual quick escape out the door, but I was stopped.

"Here's your pen. Don't want you to think I'm stealing in church. Thank you."

It was the handsome new member, and I thought, *Uh-huh, I bet he sat behind me on purpose.* "Oh, you could have kept the pen," I told him. "But you're welcome."

"I can't just call you 'pretty lady' all the time. Well, I could… but what's your name?"

The man was gorgeous, and "pretty lady" would have worked just fine coming from him. Still, I kept my words pleasant but minimal.

"You can call me Jay," I said. "Nice to meet you."

"OK, and Jay is—"

I cut him off. "Jasmine. It's short for Jasmine." I was ready to go, and I was hungry. *He's holding me up, and I don't want some woman or baby mama popping up and wondering why I'm talking to her man.* My mind had already gone into left field.

"Oh, Jasmine...like the little Disney princess in *Aladdin*. It fits you."

"Mr....um..."

"I'm sorry. I'm Richard Heart. It's nice to—"

"I'm kind of in a hurry because my stomach is talking to me. I have to grab some food."

"I could join—"

I was already headed toward my car. "Goodbye, Mr. Rich Heart!" I yelled, hurrying away. "God bless ya!" I was wearing a pencil skirt, and my hips were going left and right across that parking lot at full speed.

He shook his head and laughed. Every Sunday from then on, Richard sat either in the row behind me or in front of me. He soon decided that if he just sat beside me at church, he would not have to tap me for a pen, my Bible, paper, candy, or any of the many excuses he used to get my attention. No lady or kids ever showed up with him—no male partner either. Soon I found myself asking *him* for a pen, knowing I always had my own. Finally Richard wrote me a note on the back of a service program that said he would like to call me one day. His number was on the paper with a sloppy smiley face drawing. I burst out laughing and had to cough to play it off.

"Do you need a cough drop? You probably got Walmart in that purse," he joked.

"Since we're already in church, let me pray for you and your drawing skills. That smiley face needs a healing," I whispered. I put one hand on the smiley face and held the other up to heaven, my eyes closed tight.

He shook his head, as if to say, *OK, you got me on that one.*

One time in service, the pastor just *had* to do the "Look over and tell your neighbor you love 'em" thing. Needless to say, Richard loved that.

He wrote another note that said, *The Lord is answering my prayer, even though you haven't called me yet.*

I wrote back, *Lucky you.*

He wrote, *I don't need luck. I got Jesus,* with that same ugly little smiley face drawing. It was cute though.

Eventually I let him take me to dinner some Sundays after church, but I chose to meet him at these places. The only reason he knew where I lived is because one day I had come outside of the church parking lot to a flat tire. He changed it and offered to follow me home since I was driving on a spare. Through our many chats on the phone Richard told me that he worked in construction. This didn't bother me. He was always lots of fun and a Southern gentleman, opening doors, pulling my chair out, and blessing our food before we ate. Several months passed, and we had become friends. But February was approaching, and although I missed celebrating Valentine's Day, I didn't want to be reminded that I was single. So I asked him who his Valentine was. After he sadly answered, "Nobody," I just suggested we hang out. There was no use in the two of us being bored on that day, so at least dinner and a movie could be fun. He agreed, and it happened to be his first time going out on Valentine's Day.

"So what would you like to do, pretty lady?"

"I'm not picky but you *do* have to feed me."

"Yes indeed. I have a construction job coming up at a place you'll like."

"Awesome! Which restaurant?"

"Oh it's a casino with a…"

"Hell no…oops I mean… I don't really like casinos." I said.

He shook his head, "You ain't saved like you say you're saved."

He was laughing so hard at me. I was so embarrassed.

"We all fall short. The Lord is not through…Richard, don't judge me."

I prayed our friendship would be strong, because that was the foundation of what I really wanted and needed. When Valentine's Day came, I still wouldn't let him pick me up from my house but at the last minute I changed my mind. That was because I opened my front door and saw a pearl Mercedes limousine parked in front of my home. I couldn't argue. I was speechless. There I was informed that Richard had booked two rooms at Mandalay Bay resort and casino. *I just can't get away from the darn casino.* We arrived at a rather remote area and I could not believe what I saw. Richard was standing beside a private jet that his construction company used for infrastructure meetings around the world. During the limo ride I found out that his *construction job* was actually construction manager for multi-million dollar company where he started as a bricklayer. When he had started that job he was always in his work clothes with paint, cement, dirt and grime on them. He had tried dating but his experience wasn't great because he was a blue collar worker. He told me he never felt appreciated because, for a long time, his line of work wasn't appealing to women. Richard eventually stopped telling ladies where he worked and just concentrated on working hard and furthering his education and career. While I had been praying for my relationship recovery, he was praying to be led to his true love. One the plane we talked about how we met. I dodged Richard for a long time, because I had no intention of rushing back into a relationship or whatever it was I was doing. The difference was that we both wanted to be fixed within ourselves before trying to find a soul mate. Richard wasn't perfect, and he had a past like I did. But neither of us wanted to revisit or make excuses for our histories. It was time to move on, trust, laugh, relax, and love again. In due time, that is what happened and we became best friends. While we continued to see each other Richard wanted to know about my future career plans, and he was very interested in helping me see those through. He was already well established in finance and marketing, so I was at ease knowing he was challenging me to be greater so he could have someone to match his own ambition. We cheered each other on, and we were not afraid to serve up honest criticism.

We both needed depth and purpose in our relationship. He wasn't new to pretty faces, and neither was I. Physical intimacy had played such a negative role in our past relationships that neither of us visited the idea. Truthfully we were so absorbed with each other that we knew it would be like an explosion if we ever went there, so we just chilled out. This was a guy I could discuss a good book with, talk about future career plans with, go dancing with, or hang out in the park. I recalled how on that Valentine's Day we laughed, cried, played, and most importantly, we prayed together.

That night, at the Mandalay Bay hotel, he slept in his room and I slept in mine. The next morning we came back home just in time for church. Before I stepped foot in the sanctuary I called Ashley and apologized. She threatened to knock me out if I ever acted a fool with her again but she apologized as well. Love was back, and it was a winner-take-all scenario! In one year, I became my best friend's fiancée. He told me it didn't take men long to know if they saw themselves with a woman long term or not. Some guys just liked stringing woman along, and women did it too, he said. *I knew that all too well.* After spending much needed quality time together and doing a lot of soul searching, I became his wife. Our wedding anniversary? February 14.

House Rules

(Rules that are specific to a particular casino)

These guidelines and boundaries might help you along the path toward a healthy relationship with yourself and God. They helped me, Jasmine Jones—now Mrs. Heart—hit it big.

- **Take breaks.** When you don't take time out to be alone and figure out what went wrong, what went right, and who you are, you get lonely. Jumping from one partner to the next doesn't help you. It temporarily fills a void. More than likely, even though one person might have done something to cause a breakup, both people had flaws—yes, both people. Spend time with yourself and in prayer. God will get his time with you, even if separation from others is the result.
- **Play within a fixed budget.** You know what you will and won't take from people. Don't get into situations you

can't afford. Know your limits. There's a difference between being open-minded and being a doormat. People will do to you only what you allow. If you don't tell people upfront the issues that can't be compromised, you will pay big time. You don't have to play a role for someone who just might be playing a role for you too.

- **Keep track of your results.** When you know better, you do better. Thinking you can mimic a relationship from your past with someone who looks better, has more money, has no kids, and goes to church is crazy. It's basically saying you want a better person, but you are too selfish to be one. Even if you have to keep a journal of things said and done in a relationship that caused hurt, do that. Make a conscious effort not to do those things again, and don't accept bad behavior from decent people. Holy people cheat, lie, steal, and sometimes kill. But if you work on you, you will recognize dysfunction from a mile away. And yes, make notes about conversations and gestures that brought joy to other people and to yourself, and repeat those daily.

- **Accept a loss.** If you love someone, you really have to let him or her go. We hang on to people who were only supposed to show something so we could be prepared for the real deal. However, we act selfish and hate to be wrong, so we fight for something we were never meant to have for the long term. Before you know it, time and energy are wasted, and instead of at least maintaining a friendship, you don't even speak. You don't look at each other when you walk by—all because you didn't let go. It's perfectly all right if a relationship ended. Use the time after to focus on your purpose, your dreams, and your vision. When you do that, you never really lose out—you just move on.

- **Don't chase losses.** Delete those numbers from your phone. Remove certain people from your social media contact list. Why do you want people to have access to you if they have proven they are not an asset to you? It is not a rule that you have to remain in touch with anyone and everybody. That is not proving you are strong enough but actually shows your weakness. People often close doors but leave them unlocked on purpose in hopes something will change. These people don't mind losing, and that is a scary concept. If someone really loves you and was meant for you, he or she will come to you through God's divine intervention. If God is not in it, leave it alone.

- **Don't borrow to gamble.** Some of you, just to survive a relationship, act like the hurt or pain is not that bad. You pretend you can't do better, maybe because you know someone who was in a similar situation and stuck it out for years. Leave other folks' lives alone, and manage your own. Playing tough and hard only means your times will get tougher and harder. Soon you will look to someone else to give you what you aren't getting in your current relationship. Filling voids doesn't change your reality— without changing from within, you just stay in the same place but with another face.

- **Beware of distractions.** The biggest lesson to take away from this book is not to be envious of people who appear happier than you, have a sexier mate than yours, have more money than you, live in a bigger house, drive a nicer car... and the list goes on. If you pay attention to what God is saying to you, all elements of your life will fall into place. When you have a moment of confusion about a person, when you feel something just isn't right, when you get the urge to waste your time, and when you see for yourself that you are in a downward situation, don't let pretty faces, charming words, fit bodies, or money fool you. And if you are trying to do right, whether single or in a relationship, and anyone wants to get you off track, that is a clear sign to go the other way. People know when you are vulnerable because they are too and need to be around someone who breaks easily to fulfill their own selfish quests.

- **Learn basic strategies.** I dare you to pray over those you feel have wronged you. I dare you to admit your mistakes and pray over yourself and the person who is meant just for you—before you even meet. Chivalry is not dead. No matter how independent a woman is, she wants to know a gentleman. She wants affection, without giving hints or having to nag about it. Men want softness, even from a strong woman. Don't seek so much advice from your friends that you forget to talk with your own mate. But always consult God first. When God sees you are willing to quit playing games and let him have his way in your life, he will reveal your purpose, so focus on that before looking for romance again. Your primary obligation is to honor and love God.

- **Learn about the games you choose to play.** Just because one person put up with your craziness, that doesn't mean the next will. Some really crazy people will not rest until they retaliate. You can learn about whom you are dealing with when you meet his or her closest friends and family. Although we can't put people in a box, you don't stand in rain without getting wet. What does this mean? The person you date will be around people he relates to or with whom he has rapport. While scoping the scene on other people, be honest about who you are and where you come from, and do some inner cleansing. I know some say opposites attract, but in fact, like attracts like. Souls recognize one another, so it is very important that you practice the same qualities you require in a partner. If you have a list of characteristics you want in a mate, you should also have a list of qualities *you* want to have as a partner.

- **Play from the specific bankroll.** Sometimes we stay with people, promising to leave after one more incident. And then they do two or three more things, but we stay. When you have given all you have to a person or are fed up, don't dismiss how you feel by pretending to be patient. The deeper you get into something you know isn't right, the harder it is to find your way back out of the unhealthy pattern.

- **Know when to cash out.** Honestly, some of you knew from day one that there would be time limits on certain relationships. You let the enemy trick you into thinking you were a bad person if you cut ties. The enemy told you that you were judging people, but it was simply God giving you discernment. When you constantly think about being treated better, when you know you can treat yourself better, when you are losing yourself to gain what you think is love, when you are running out of time, when you haven't even talked to God because you are embarrassed that you wasted so much time in a lie, when you are hurting more than you are happy, when you sob more than you smile, when you feel pain more often than you feel power, when you feel jealousy instead of joy, when someone is not even investing in loving you the way you deserve…it is over. Give it to God with a prayer that he will restore, replenish, revive, rebuild, recondition, repair, reestablish, and renew every magnificent thing about you. That is where your jackpot is—being who God called you to be. It is priceless, and if you stop gambling away the very things that make you wonderful, strong, and valuable, then winning is inevitable!

If you must play, decide upon three things at the start: the rules of the game, the stakes, and the quitting time.

—*Chinese Proverb*

≈The End≈

A Special Note from Jasmine Jones

To win in love, I needed the desire to win in life. I also had to stop playing games. Even if you are trying to do things right, when you participate in a game you know you can't win, you are at fault too. My spirit had to heal before my heart could. I had to learn from my mistakes and stop wanting what looked fine on the surface…because everything that glitters ain't gold. I admit that with every new face, I hit up every corner of the love casino, dropping all the wrong pieces of myself in the slut machine—oh, I mean *slot* machine—and wondering why I was never able to cash out. However, when I let God call the shots, I hit it big. I am in love, and all the pieces of me are back in place. It was challenging to give anything to the one who deserved when I felt I'd lost parts of me myself to those who didn't. I can truly say I got Jasmine back, and God gave me a new "Heart." I still call my husband Mr. Rich because he is a valuable treasure to me. He calls me Jackpot Jasmine because he says with me he is set for life.